Touch me Gently

J.R. LOVELESS

Dreamspinner Press

Published by
Dreamspinner Press
4760 Preston Road
Suite 244-149
Frisco, TX 75034
http://www.dreamspinnerpress.com/

Cover Art by Anne Cain   annecain.art@gmail.com
Cover Design by Mara McKennen

ISBN: 978-1-61581-574-6

Printed in the United States of America
First Edition
September, 2010

eBook edition available
eBook ISBN: 978-1-61581-575-3

To all my readers of Aarinfantasy,
you gave me inspiration and hope when I needed it most.

CHAPTER 1

HANDS grabbed at him, holding him down roughly. His clothes were stripped from his body, torn as threads gave way at the harsh tugging. His pleading for it to stop flooded the room and then screams of agony as he felt his body being violated. The musky scent of sweat and alcohol reached his nostrils, and he gagged as he lay there beneath the unforgiving, thrusting body above his. His mind seemed to shut down, and he felt nothing, heard nothing, was nothing. Fingers bit into his flesh, digging deep and bruising it. Suddenly, hot warmth flooded his insides, and the body above his collapsed.

Before he could try to move, a searing pain split one side of his face, and he screamed again as blood spilled down his face, filling his nose and mouth, choking his cries off. He coughed over and over, trying to keep the coppery liquid from filling his lungs. "Now, no one will want you! You'll always be mine!"

Kaden James shot upright in bed, gasping for breath, his body sweating profusely and soaking the sheets around him. Terror pounded through him as he remembered what he had tried so hard to forget. His violet eyes wandered around the shabby one-room apartment he rented, searching for any demons hidden in the

1

shadows. He slumped back down onto the bed, struggling to control his breathing and to stem the flood of terror. That day's events had opened the door to his memories again. Nineteen now, he lived alone, and today he'd been fired from another job. Fear of large men always ended up getting him fired because he couldn't control his panic attacks. Sighing, Kaden ran a thin, shaking hand over his face. Knowing he wouldn't be able to go back to sleep, he rolled out of bed to make himself a cup of coffee.

He flicked on a light and wandered over to the sink to fill the coffeepot with water. He set it to brew and sat down to wait, lighting up a cigarette. The apartment he lived in was all that he could afford, dingy and small with only one room that consisted of the kitchen, the bedroom, and a small adjoining bathroom that you could barely turn around in. His hand lifted to trace the ugly scar that ran from the corner of his left eye in a curve down to the corner of his mouth. No one wanted to hire him for anything other than grunt work because of his face. Most people found it difficult not to stare and wonder or be disgusted and turn away. Tomorrow he would have to go back to the labor agency and see if they had anything else for him. The manager had to be getting tired of him, but he couldn't change the deep-seated fear that crippled him and sent him to his knees.

The coffee finished brewing as he stubbed out his cigarette, and he grabbed the only mug he owned, rinsed it out, and filled it with piping hot coffee. Sniffing appreciatively, he took a hesitant sip, wincing when it burned the tip of his tongue. He'd always been slender and almost feminine in some ways. His shoulder-length black hair, shaggy around his face, gave him an even more feminine appearance. It attracted men in a way he didn't want. He might look tiny, only five foot six, but he was strong physically due to the many jobs he'd taken requiring heavy lifting. Despite the muscle he'd gained from those jobs, he still cowered when faced with dominating males. Emotionally unstable from everything that had happened in his life, he tried his best not to let those thoughts and memories control him.

Dawn spreading across the sky, Kaden rose to shower and dress in one of the few outfits he owned. Locking his door behind him, deadbolt and all, he trudged down the stairs, stepping around the drunken bum that lay at the bottom. The area he resided in couldn't be considered the most sanitary, nor the safest, but it was cheap and the only thing he could afford. Traffic had already started flowing heavily along the streets of New York City as he slowly wound his way through the crowds of passersby toward the labor agency. When he arrived, he gave Terry Reynolds, the manager, a tentative smile.

"I don't know what I'm going to do with you, kid," Terry admonished quietly. He didn't know the kid's story but he knew something bad had happened to him. The haunted look that shadowed the boy's eyes told him that much at least.

"How many jobs has that been in three weeks? Five? Let me see if I have anything else," he said with a sigh, and Kaden gave him a grateful look, plopping down into one of the cracked vinyl chairs in the front office while Terry wandered back into his own.

Thirty minutes went by before Terry returned to the front office. He'd come up with a great idea, at least he hoped Kaden thought so. "Listen, Kaden, would you be willing to get out of the city?"

"What?" Kaden asked, his voice hoarse. He didn't use it much. No friends and fear of strangers kept him silent a good portion of the time.

"Well, I know you have trouble with big groups of people, but my cousin needs someone on his ranch in Montana. To cook and clean. Can you cook?"

Kaden stared at him in surprise. He was an excellent cook, if he thought so himself. He loved to cook and had been doing so since he was twelve. "I... don't know what they would think. I like to think I'm a pretty good cook. But... Montana?" The idea suddenly appealed to him, getting out of the city and away from the huge crowds of people.

"It's only for three months, though. After that, you'd have to find something else. You see, he has a lot more workers and ranch hands coming in during the next few months because of roundup season and all. So he needs someone who can make food and lots of it. Can I trust you to do this, kid?" Terry asked him softly.

Kaden nodded and then looked down at his hands. "What about my apartment?"

"You'll have to let it go. But if anything, when the three months are up, you can stay with me until you find another one," Terry offered eagerly.

"Will your cousin mind that I'm a... guy?" Kaden asked quietly.

"I already called him. He knows you're a guy and doesn't care as long as you can cook. It's not like you're going to be sleeping with him or anything."

Kaden's head shot up and his eyes widened with panic, but Terry's words sank in, and he nodded. "All right. I guess that'll be fine."

"Good. You'll leave tomorrow. There'll be a plane ticket waiting for you at the airport," Terry told him.

He stood up jerkily, unsure of what the hell he had just gotten himself into, and headed back to his apartment to pack up the very minor belongings he had. There were few personal items since the apartment had been partially furnished when he rented it. The only things he had to take with him included several articles of clothing, the coffeepot, and the journals that he wrote lyrics in. He loved to write songs, beautiful heartbreaking songs. Something to get his

4

fears out, and his desire to be loved, even though he knew that would never happen because of the emotional and physical scars he carried.

The next day, as he stood waiting in line at the counter, his duffel bag on the floor beside him, Kaden sensed the curious stares at the scar on his face, and he bit his lip to stop himself from yelling at the strangers to leave him alone. It always happened that way. No matter where he went, people stared at the grotesqueness of his face. The line moved, and then he arrived at the front to claim his ticket. He showed his ID and moments later he sat waiting at the gate for his flight to be called. Taking out the black and white composition book that looked ragged from a lot of use, he started to write. He had almost finished the song by the time they called his flight, and he completed it on the way out to Montana. He wound up falling asleep partway there only to be brought awake by one of the flight attendants shaking his shoulder because he'd started crying in his sleep. He gave her a pained smile and shook his head when she asked if he needed anything.

When Kaden arrived, he stepped out into the airport and looked around, spotting the turnstile baggage claim. He strode forward and looked for his blue duffel bag. He heard a voice behind him call his name by the time the bag reached him. He snatched it up and turned around to find a man a little shorter than himself standing there and looking around the airport. "I'm Kaden James," he said as he approached the man, waiting to see the same curious stare at his scar, but to his surprise that wasn't what happened at all.

Instead the little man cracked a smile at him, causing his tan weathered face to crease even further, and his blue eyes twinkled at him merrily. "I'm Charlie. Logan's foreman. Is that all you have?" he asked, frowning at the bag in Kaden's hands.

"Yeah," Kaden said without explanation.

"Okay. Let's get going. So did you have any trouble on the flight?" The little man led him toward a red beat-up pickup truck just outside the doors of the airport.

Kaden tossed the bag into the back of the truck and slid into the passenger seat. "It went fine."

"Not much of a talker, hmm? That's a good thing, I guess, since you'll be in the house by yourself most of the day," Charlie replied, starting the truck.

The drive from the airport to the ranch took about forty-five minutes to an hour. Kaden listened to the little man ramble on as he drove and injected one or two word sentences here and there.

"Ah, we're here," Charlie crowed, pulling into a dirt driveway leading to the ranch.

Kaden stared around him curiously, wondering what type of ranch it was. White-washed fences lined the dirt road, and he could see several men in the distance, some on horses and others on foot. Fear stuck in his throat at the sight of so many men, but he coughed and managed to ask, "Cows or horses?"

"Cows. Logan has horses for the roundup and all, but he raises steers. Ah, there he is, over by the corral there." Charlie pointed out a tall man in a denim shirt, faded blue jeans, and a black cowboy hat standing with his back to the driveway. Kaden swallowed nervously when he saw how big the man appeared even from there.

He slowly climbed out of the truck, grabbing his bag from the bed. He winced when he heard Charlie shout, "Logan! Hey, Logan!" Charlie waved his hat to get the cowboy's attention, and Logan started walking toward them.

His anxiety increased tenfold the closer the man got. At least a foot taller than Kaden, he caused Kaden's heart to beat even harder against his ribcage when he realized how far up he had to look. What the hell had he been thinking? The man oozed sexuality and danger—nice muscular build, dazzling green eyes, and sandy blond hair, cut ragged, like it had been done with a pair of blunt scissors. His skin seemed almost as tan as boot leather, with fine lines around the corners of his eyes and along the backs of his hands. He had a long-legged stride that ate up the ground between them in seconds.

"You're a tiny thing, ain't ya," Logan drawled as he drew near. He stuck out his hand in greeting. "Logan Michaels." He frowned at the haunted look in the boy's eyes, and how it took the younger man a moment to respond. His eyes were instantly drawn to the scar on his face, unable to imagine what could have left such a mark on the soft, white skin.

Kaden slowly and reluctantly placed his hand in Logan's. It felt as though Logan's hand virtually swallowed his whole, and he jerked it back quickly. "K-Kaden James."

"Come on. I'll show you the house." Logan strode up the porch steps, shaking his head at why a slender teenager like this boy would be interested in burying himself on a ranch for three months. His cousin hadn't told him much, just that the teen desperately needed a job, so he'd said okay.

"I hope you can cook, because otherwise you'll have a whole group of angry men after you," he teased gently to try and get the kid to relax.

A small sound of terror escaped Kaden before he could stop it, and Logan came to an abrupt halt, turning back to look at him. "That was a joke, kid," he said soothingly, his eyes taking in the absolute panic in the boy's face. "Can you cook?"

Kaden nodded, only relaxing slightly. "Yes. I've been cooking since I was twelve."

Logan gave a short nod before continuing into the house,

Kaden hesitantly following. "This is the kitchen. All of the foodstuffs are in the pantry there. Now, there are twenty men on the ranch, and you'll need to make enough to feed them all. Understand?"

"Yes." At the mention of the number of men on the ranch, Kaden once again berated himself for being so stupid to come to a place like this without knowing anyone here. Not that he'd really known anyone back in New York aside from Terry.

"Good. Now, whenever you need to restock just make up a list, and I'll send Charlie into town to get everything. There's very little to do here at night, so I hope you don't mind the slow pace. I'll show you where you'll be sleeping." Logan indicated that Kaden should follow him and led him down a hallway on the first floor to a room in the back.

Kaden's eyes widened in shock. He guessed the room to be about the same size as his apartment, and the bathroom was at least three times the size of the postage stamp he'd had to bear with. "Wow," he said in awe, unaware of Logan's small smile at his wonder.

"You'll have to make breakfast, lunch, and dinner. Breakfast is at 5 a.m. You'll need to prepare boxed lunches for the men to take since they'll be eating out on the trail. Except for tomorrow. We'll still be branding and castrating the steers already brought in. Dinner is usually around six. Make sure to have everything ready by then. Lunch is already over for the day so you'll only have to make dinner tonight. I would suggest you get started once you've got all your things put away, since it's already two." Logan watched the boy wandering around the room just looking at things. Amusing, yet sad at the same time, it seemed that it had been a long time since the boy had been in a nice place. That fact made his heart wrench with sympathy and pity. "I've got to get back out there. But we'll be back in at six."

"Okay," Kaden replied watching the large man leave. He quickly put away the few clothes he had, set the duffel bag, still containing the coffeepot, into the closet, and put his songbook on the bed before closing the door and heading out to the kitchen.

The pantry contained more food than he'd seen in his entire life outside of a grocery store, and he wandered through the room looking over the contents. After deciding on what would be the easiest to make in bulk, Kaden immediately lost himself in the love he had for cooking. By five thirty, he'd covered the table with huge steaming plates of fried chicken and three baskets of biscuits. Three giant dishes of mashed potatoes and a big pot of gravy sat on the sideboard next to the dining room table. He'd also made a huge pan of apple cobbler for dessert, currently staying warm in the oven. He tensed at the sound of men's voices as they approached the house, and he backed up into the kitchen, trying to remain hidden.

Logan wondered how the kid had fared, but he needn't have feared. The moment they came close to the house, his mouth began to water from the smell of the food waiting for them. His eyes opened wide in surprise at the sight of the steaming piles of food on the dining room table, and the men stopped speaking as they filed into the house, their own mouths dropping open. "Whoooweeee. Would you look at that?"

Kaden grinned at the man's words but stayed inside the doorway, listening to the sounds of chairs scraping the wooden floor and silverware hitting the dishes. Once the men had settled down to eat, Kaden turned on the faucet, letting the sink fill up and piled the pots and pans next to it.

Logan entered the kitchen to see Kaden standing by the sink. "Congratulations, kid." He gave a broad smile which dimmed quickly at the wariness that flooded the boy's features. "I... uh... think you're going to work out just fine. Why don't you sit at the table with us?"

The teenager shook his head furiously and began edging his way down the hallway leading to his bedroom. "There's apple cobbler in the oven, warming. Uh... I'm not really hungry right now. I'll get something a little later." Suddenly the teenager disappeared, and Logan sighed in frustration.

He made up a plate for his confusing cook, and after wrapping a paper towel over it, placed it in the microwave until later before grabbing his own food. The men were practically licking the bottom of the plates by the time dinner finished. He pulled out the apple cobbler and cut two pieces, one for him and one for the boy, before setting it on the dining room table. "Man, boss, I don't know where you found this person, but this is the best cooking I've tasted since I lived with my mama," one cowhand said, enthusiastically licking his fork.

Logan laughed and nodded in agreement. It amazed him how someone that young could have such a way with cooking. It killed him not to be able to ask questions about Kaden's past. Terry hadn't known much when he'd asked before he'd agreed to hire him. The men brought their dishes into the kitchen, piling them neatly by the sink for washing. Logan waited until the last man left before walking down to the boy's room and knocking lightly. He heard muffled sounds of movement inside before the door opened. Kaden blinked up at him, caution still lurking in those beautiful violet eyes. He didn't know why it bothered him so much that the boy seemed so afraid of him, but it rankled something fierce. "They're gone. I saved you some food since I knew it wouldn't last long with the men."

"Th-thank you," Kaden stuttered, amazed that the man had thought of him. "I'll do the dishes first."

"No. Eat first," Logan insisted, turning to walk back toward the kitchen. He'd saved his apple cobbler to eat with the teen so he could have an excuse to be able to talk to him. He heard Kaden slowly following him down the hall. "Your plate is in the

10

microwave."

Kaden took out the plate and sat down at the table, almost moaning in dismay when Logan pulled out the seat across from him. He removed the paper towel, setting it aside, then picked up the piece of chicken, and began daintily eating. He tried to ignore the older man but wasn't very successful.

Logan watched the way the boy ate, the tiny pink tongue flicking out to catch the small pieces of fried coating that stuck to his lips. It made him feel very warm, which confused him even more. He'd never been attracted to a man before, and he'd always been able to get any woman he wanted. In fact, he had a date that Friday night with Helen Chambers from the local beauty salon. Although he never intended to get married. He'd nixed the idea of marriage starting at the age of five as he watched his parents go through fight after fight.

"So, Kaden, how come you decided to come all the way out here to work?" Logan asked curiously, propping his chin in his hand.

Stiffening, Kaden wanted nothing more than to tell the man to mind his own business. "I needed a job. This was the only one available."

"I'm sure you could have found something in the city. There isn't much partying going on around these parts," Logan drawled, not noticing Kaden starting to get agitated.

"I didn't come here to party," Kaden said, standing abruptly to go do the dishes.

"I didn't mean to upset you," Logan apologized hesitantly, noticing the teen's stiff shoulders and posture.

"I'm not one for parties, Mr. Michaels. I came to do a job." The dishes clattered as Kaden rearranged them, stacking them according to size for washing. He set his jaw in a firm line, stifling

11

his anger that the cowboy believed he liked to party.

"It's Logan. I hate being called Mr. Michaels. Too reminiscent of my father." Logan grimaced at the thought and stood up, stepping close to Kaden to place his plate on the counter beside the sink.

Kaden felt the man come up next to him and flinched reflexively, causing him to drop the glass he held in his hand, watching in horror as it shattered in the sink. "I'm sorry. I'm sorry," he whimpered immediately, bringing his arms up to cover his head.

Logan stared in shock at the teenager's reaction, but instead of commenting he decided it would be best to ignore the situation for the moment and began to pick up the pieces. "It's all right. They're cheap glasses, anyway."

Surprise streaked through Kaden. Logan didn't seem to be upset. "But... I broke it," he said in confusion, letting his arms fall to his sides as he watched Logan pick up the pieces.

"Eh. I've broken almost one a day since I can remember," Logan joked, tossing the pieces in the garbage and running the faucet to rinse the tiny shards down the drain. "I'll dry while you wash, okay?"

Kaden nodded and moved to finish washing the dishes. His head whirled with all of the events of the day. He managed to relax a little as he worked side-by-side with Logan. He'd been so sure that the man would hit him for breaking the glass, but when he'd been so nonchalant and easygoing about it, his bewilderment deepened. Kaden's stomach twisted painfully, and he finished up the dishes before fleeing the kitchen, tossing a muttered good-night to the large man.

CHAPTER 2

THE next morning, Kaden got out of bed at three thirty to start breakfast and had heaping piles of scrambled eggs, pancakes, waffles, and home fries, along with toast and grits, waiting for the men when they arrived. One of the men caught sight of him as he skirted back into the kitchen and trailed after him, propping one shoulder on the doorjamb to watch Kaden move around the kitchen. "So you're the one who has been making all this delicious food," he drawled, looking appreciatively over the small form from behind.

Kaden squeaked in alarm, swinging around to face the tall man before stuttering, "Y-yes."

The man, though not as big as Logan, towered over Kaden. He had small brown eyes that seemed to run leeringly over his body, making him swallow hard with disgust as bile rose in his throat. A red stripe ran across his forehead where the cowboy hat rested during the day. Kaden cautiously kept one eye on the stranger as he started to wash the pots and pans from that morning's breakfast. Sounds of the men arriving filtered through to the kitchen, and the man pushed away from the doorway.

"Name's Franklin Williams. What's yours?" he asked, moving a little closer, his eyes watching the way the boy trembled slightly. He licked his lips as he continued toward him. The trembling increased, and it caused his dick to harden, pressing against the tight zipper of his jeans. Franklin felt like a fox hunting a rabbit, scenting the fear wafting from its prey.

"K-Kaden James," he mumbled back, edging further away each time the man took a step.

"Well, Kaden James, for a guy, you're certainly easy on the eyes," Franklin murmured as he pushed closer to the boy while running the tip of one finger down Kaden's pale forearm in an unwanted caress. "How about you and I spend some time together real soon? I could show you pleasures you've never dreamed of."

Franklin leaned forward to try and capture his lips, but Kaden turned his head and tried to get away, much to the man's anger. Eyes narrowing at the rebuff, he sniffed at the delicate neck before him. "You smell good, boy. Maybe I'll just have you for breakfast instead."

Logan approached the dining room, grinning when he heard the men all talking appreciatively. The sound of a dish dropping in the kitchen caught his attention, and he turned that way instead of going into the dining room. He immediately took in the scene before him. A dish lay in pieces on the floor, Kaden cowering against the counter, and Franklin stood leaning over him suggestively, one hand on Kaden's tiny waist.

"Franklin," Logan barked harshly, his eyes glittering dangerously. "Get your breakfast down and get to work," he snarled in warning, and the man backed away like his feet were on fire.

"S-sure thing, Boss." Franklin scurried from the room quickly.

Kaden breathed deeply. Pure panic raced through his veins. He barely registered Logan's approach, or the man's movements to pick up the dish. Memories ransacked his mind and body, leaving him a shivering, quivering mess. "Kaden?" He heard that deep voice, and he whined, raising his arms to protect his head while waiting for blows that never came.

"Hey, what's all this? I'm not going to hit you. Shh. Just relax." That liquid honey voice washed over him in tenderness, surprise and caring reflected deep inside, something Kaden hadn't heard in a long time. He felt the man's hand come to rest on his shoulder and shuddered, a mewling cry issuing from his throat.

Logan felt his chest tighten with pity and some other undefined emotion. If he hadn't already guessed previously, Logan would have known for certain at that moment that the teenager had been abused and large men terrified him. He backed away carefully. "Kaden," he called sharply, trying to get the boy's attention.

The piercing sound brought Kaden to his senses, and he realized that he'd almost lost it again. He closed his eyes in shame. "I'm sorry. Do you want me to leave?"

"What? No. Don't forget lunch is at noon," Logan stated calmly before leaving the kitchen.

Kaden escaped to the solitude of his bedroom and lay on the bed staring at the ceiling. His body still trembled from the overload of terror, and a headache began to form behind his eyes. Not even a full day here, and he'd already been close to having a panic attack. His fists clenched in the sheets around him as he felt tears prick the corners of his eyes. Rolling into a ball, he pulled his knees up to his chest and wrapped his arms around them. He didn't want to disappoint Terry or Logan and that surprised him. Though only there sixteen hours, he cared what Logan thought. Finally, he managed to sit up without the urge to throw up and carefully climbed off the bed, stumbling back toward the kitchen to finish the dishes from that morning and start lunch.

For lunch, he started making huge mile-high sandwiches and a big heaping bowl of potato salad for the guys. Once they were made, he set them back inside the fridge until later and started to clean up the dining room area. A large table sat in the middle of the room with dozens of chairs piled around it, and the sideboard rested on the wall closest to the door leading into the kitchen. The walls, painted white, had very few decorations, just small paintings here or there.

The living room appeared to be a comfortable area and the most used. Two large overstuffed couches, well-worn from longtime use, took up most of the space. A wooden coffee table sat in front of those couches, scarred and beaten. A fireplace dominated one wall, a rocking and easy chair nearby, along with a bookshelf taking up another wall. He wandered over and read over the titles. He enjoyed reading because it gave him ideas for his songs and an escape from reality. Though Kaden had filled the notebook with them, he'd never shown his lyrics to anyone before. Shyness and apprehension of his own disappointment kept his hopes leashed tightly inside him.

He moved to the fireplace to look at the pictures on the mantel curiously. There were pictures of men he hadn't met, but he did recognize the ones of Logan. He picked one up and studied it. Logan looked young in the picture, and stood proudly holding the reins of a big black horse. Everything about the tall cowboy reminded him of a lion: the air of confidence that surrounded him, the rippling muscles when he moved, the sandy blond mane, and even the graceful way he carried himself. His finger traced over the strong features, and he sighed, placing it back on the mantel. He could never have a normal relationship even if he wanted to. His anxiety would always ruin everything.

Deciding to clean while he waited for the men to come in for lunch, he threw himself into dusting, sweeping, and mopping. His mind shut down while he worked, and by the time he heard the

16

scraping of boots along the porch, the dining room, kitchen, and living room fairly sparkled in the early afternoon sunlight. Kaden hurriedly set the sandwiches, plates, silverware, and the bowl of potato salad on the table before making his escape to his bedroom. He heard the chairs being pulled out from the table, and then laughing and joking. Deep voices hummed through the wood of his bedroom door.

It didn't take long before there came a knock at his door, and he flinched, wondering if Logan had changed his mind. He wearily stood up from where he'd been sitting on the floor, his lyric book next to him, to open the door. Logan stood there holding a plate and a tall glass of milk in his hand. "I brought you something to eat before the men eat it all," Logan explained huskily, his eyes taking in the dark circles beneath Kaden's eyes and slipping past him to the composition book lying on the floor.

Kaden hesitantly took the food from Logan. "Thank you," he whispered, still not able to look into those gorgeous green eyes.

A gasp jumped from his throat when a strong finger slid beneath his chin to lift his head. "If any of my men ever bother you again, you come tell me, okay? And I'll deal with it," Logan instructed him sternly, his expression serious.

Kaden swallowed nervously but nodded, feeling the calloused rough skin of that finger rubbing against the sensitive skin underneath his chin. It left a tingling sensation behind when Logan pulled away. His eyes immediately dropped to his feet before he spoke. "I'm sorry I broke another dish."

Logan rammed his fist into his jeans pocket, trying to erase the feeling left behind by the kid's soft skin. He didn't know what came over him or possessed him to touch the boy. He didn't even know why he'd been so angry that morning to see Franklin near him. It left him confused, and he didn't like feeling off balance. "It's okay," he said gruffly before spinning on his heel and walking away.

Kaden gazed after him until Logan disappeared around the corner. Then he slowly closed his door and returned to his seat on the floor. He set the plate on the nightstand, not hungry in the least after the upset that morning. The side of the bed dug into his back, but he picked up his notebook to start writing again. After a while, the house quieted down, and he could hear the men shouting out in the corrals once again. He stood up and stretched, yawning as he shuffled to the kitchen. He cleaned up the dishes piled neatly beside the sink, drying them and putting them away for the next meal. When he finished, he wasn't sure what he wanted to do. He gazed out the window and caught sight of a big white horse in one of the corrals outside. Curiosity made his feet move, and within moments, he stood outside the fence, watching the horse prance around the enclosed area. It snorted as it trotted near him, yet not close enough for him to reach out and touch.

It eyed him warily, moving restlessly along the enclosure. It seemed to be unhappy about being in there. "I know how you feel," he muttered, moving closer to place his hands on the fence. "Trapped. Like you'll never be free again."

The horse seemed to nod at his words and gingerly moved a little closer to him. Kaden smiled and rested his chin on his hands on top of the fencing. He watched the horse dancing and running. He kept creeping closer and closer to where Kaden stood. Before long the animal came within reach, nibbling at his hair. For the first time in years, he laughed as it tickled him, the sound foreign to him. The stallion neighed and bumped his nose against Kaden's cheek. Kaden carefully raised a hand to its forehead and started to rub there. The horse snorted again, causing Kaden to jump slightly. He stayed watching the animal for a while longer, enjoying the undemanding, non-frightening company.

Not long after, he returned to the kitchen to start the preparations for dinner. He decided to go with something easy and made two huge pans of lasagna, three large bowls of Caesar salad, and garlic rolls that he made from scratch. The kitchen smelled wonderful from the scent of the food cooking, and it permeated the house, drifting out of the open windows. Involved in his cooking, Kaden didn't hear the front door open and shut, or the sound of booted feet moving through the house. He let out a small cry of alarm when a voice spoke behind him.

"Well, Logan's done gone and got himself a fancy chef," a female voice drawled, and he jerked around to find a girl about his age standing in the doorway. She grinned at his surprise. "I suppose he hasn't told you about me."

"N-no," Kaden stammered, studying the girl in front of him. She was very pretty, with waist-length blonde hair pulled back in a braid that hung over one shoulder at the moment, and big green eyes twinkling with amusement. Her lips were a dusty red, and the grin only made them seem more perfect.

"I'm Shea. Shea Michaels. His sister." She stepped further into the kitchen, holding out her hand, and he took it lightly, shaking it gently before releasing her.

"I'm Kaden," he returned warily. He didn't fear women, but he wasn't all together comfortable around them, either. He didn't have experience with the opposite sex in any way. That, and he lacked the confidence to try because of the scar on his face.

"Well, Kaden. I heard Logan went and got himself a cook, but I'm surprised you turned out to be a guy. And here I thought I had a chance at a girl friend." She sighed dramatically, batting her eyelashes at him and giggling playfully.

His eyes widened, and he blushed brightly, red creeping up his neck and along his cheeks, making his scar stand out even more. "I… I'm sorry."

"Don't apologize." She sniffed appreciatively. "If it tastes as good as it smells, I'm not disappointed you're a guy at all. 'Course, I'm sure Logan is, since it's been a long time since he got lucky." She cracked up at that, not noticing Kaden's sudden tension. "Do you need help with anything?"

"No, thank you. I only have to make the dessert now." His thoughts were stuck on her words about Logan being disappointed about his gender. He didn't know why that idea bothered him so much, but it almost seemed to hurt. Shoving the feeling away roughly, along with the other thoughts that plagued him, he smiled weakly and moved around her to find the ingredients for the apple pies he intended to make.

"So, Kaden, do you like to dance?" she asked, leaning her elbows on the island counter in the middle of the kitchen.

"I don't know how," he admitted reluctantly as he started to put together the pie crusts.

"You what?" she demanded, pushing away from the counter. "You've never danced before? Line dancing, slow dancing, nothing?" Her astonishment made him feel embarrassed.

To cover it up, he just shrugged and continued on with his preparations.

"Well, while you're here, we'll have to change that. I'm taking you out on Friday night. To Jackson's Bar just off the highway. They have some of the best honky-tonk this side of the Mississippi."

"I… I don't know. I'm only here to work. Not have fun," he protested, his mind wandering back to Logan's words yesterday. The man assumed he liked to party, and if he went out with Shea it would seem like he'd lied to the man. Shea was also Logan's sister. He doubted that Logan would want a messed-up guy like Kaden involved with his sister. "I don't think it would be a good idea."

"Pshh. If you're worried about my brother not approving, don't be. He knows I can handle myself. Besides you're too scrawny to be able to take advantage of me. I'm built like a race horse, with the muscles too." She swept her braid back over her shoulder and continued. "Not only that, you're not really my type. I like guys taller than me. Sorry." She gave him an apologetic look, which he just grunted at. It didn't bother him.

Shea didn't leave. She stayed in the kitchen with him, talking to him even though he didn't really talk back. With her being a chatterbox it made him the perfect companion. "Hey, Kaden?"

"Yeah," he replied, wiping down the counters and setting the timer for the pies.

"How'd you get that scar?" she asked curiously.

Kaden stiffened. His entire body just froze in place, and he squeezed his eyes shut tight. His attempt to repress the memories failed, and they beat at him, opening the emotional wounds that had never healed and making the physical ones, though long-since healed, throb in remembrance.

"Kaden?" Her warm voice seemed to come from a long way off, down a long tunnel. Warm and concerned. "Kaden? Are you all right?" She placed a hand on his shoulder and shook him slightly.

Even though subconsciously he knew the hand belonged to Shea, he couldn't stop himself from dropping to the floor and curling into a ball, waiting for the beating he anticipated. "Jesus! Kaden? What's wrong? Oh my God."

She dropped to her knees next to him and started to rub his back comfortingly. "Come on, Kaden," she crooned, her voice soft and mellow as she tried to talk him out of whatever place he'd gone to. "It's all right. You don't have to tell me. I'm sorry I asked. Hey, uh… do you want me to teach you how to ride? That would be cool, huh? Or you can teach me how to cook. I'm terrible at that. I'd burn water, or so Logan tells me constantly."

Shea just started to ramble on about things—her school work and the dorm she lived in, her friends and what she wanted to do with her life. The attack started to ebb as he listened to her soft, pleasant voice and the way it flowed smoothly over his body and mind. The throbbing stopped, and the emotional wounds began to knit themselves back together for the time being. Eventually he became aware of everything around him, shame at his loss of control due to such a small thing cascading over him. "I… I'm sorry," he whispered, his fingers twisting together.

She gently placed her hands on his, stopping the panicky, frantic movements. "It's all right. Hey, we all have things to bear, right? Ah. I think the bell dinged for your pies, Kaden."

Shea watched the skinny teenager drag himself up from the ground, not moving from where she kneeled. Pity for the boy engulfed her. It saddened her to see someone so fragile because of abuse. It also disgusted her that others could harm someone in such a way, uncaring that it left more than physical scars on the outside. "So are we on for dancing on Friday night?"

Kaden still hesitated, and then gave a jerky nod, hoping he hadn't made a mistake. "Sure," he said in a thin voice, keeping his face away from her.

A squeal issued from her, and she suddenly hugged him from behind, taking him by surprise. Her arms wrapped around his chest, and she squeezed him tightly for a split second. "I'll make sure you have fun. Okay, Kaden?" She practically bounced from the room, and he shook his head, a small smile lurking around the corners of his mouth.

Kaden had everything ready and on the table when the men arrived for dinner. Once again, he vanished into his room. Disappointment flared inside Logan, so sharp that it astonished him.

"Logan!" He heard his name shouted happily, and a figure launched itself at him. He caught her and whirled her around.

"Hey, kiddo! I didn't know you were due in today," he chastised her affectionately.

"I wanted to surprise you." She smiled happily up at him. "So how goes the roundup, big brother?"

"Not too bad, and coming back to food like this doesn't hurt, either." He breathed deeply, dragging the scent of the food into his nostrils.

"Yeah, I met your new cook," she replied in a hushed tone. "Logan... I think there's something seriously tragic in his past."

"I noticed," he returned in an even lower tone. "But it's not our place to ask. You know that. If he wants to talk about it, I'm sure he will. So how's school going?" he asked, changing the subject to a more neutral topic.

She sat down at the table to eat, laughing and joking with the men. Most of them had known her from the time she was a baby, and they'd watched her grow up alongside Logan. They treated her like their own daughter or sister. Much to her dismay, when it came to a certain cowhand, but no matter what she did, the cowhand rebuffed her advances. Her mind kept drifting back to Kaden. Maybe if she befriended him, he would open up. Then again, maybe not. If just the thought of his past could do such damage to him, what would actually talking about it do?

The men finished dinner quickly, starving after the long hours out in the sun. Logan wondered if the kid had eaten and stood up to go find out, but his sister beat him to the punch. "I'm going to take him something to eat. He didn't eat anything yet, and I'm sure he's starving," Shea said, taking a plate that she'd already made up for Kaden from the microwave.

He lifted an eyebrow at her, and she glared at him. "What? He has to eat, too, and I know how those guys get when it comes to good food, so I put some away for him."

"Don't get too attached, Shea," he warned, and then he scowled as he realized that he needed to take his own advice.

CHAPTER 3

KADEN sat huddled against the headboard, his arms around his knees as he gazed out the window at the moon rising high into the sky. Its soft glow drifted down to touch the rich earth outside his window. Why had he come here in the first place? Why didn't he just die that day instead of living? If you could even call his weak hold on his existence actually living. If he'd given in and just let go that day, he wouldn't be causing trouble for the people around him. Terry, who had been nothing but nice to him from the day he'd walked into the labor office. Shea, who'd comforted him so easily even though she didn't know a damn thing about him. And then there was Logan, someone who was so big, so intimidating, yet seemed so gentle and caring. The skin underneath his chin tingled in reminder of that simple touch that afternoon, and he rubbed at it, trying to make it go away.

A delicate knock sounded on his door, and he stood up, dizziness swamping him for a breath of a second, but he shook it off and moved toward the door. Surprisingly, Shea stood there holding a plate and a glass of soda for him. "Here." She thrust them at him. "I saved you some food before the hungry herds could gulp it all down."

She brushed past him into his room without waiting for an invite and started looking around. Nothing really personal sat out any place, and she pouted mentally. She'd been hoping for an idea on his past.

He set the plate and the drink on the nightstand, perching on the edge of the bed uneasily as he watched her walk around the room. He got the impression she was looking for something, but he didn't have anything, except his lyrics. The smell of the food made him nauseous, and he wanted nothing more than to toss it in the garbage. Aside from the emotional issues he dealt with on a daily basis, Kaden barely ate. Most of the time, he couldn't stomach the thought of eating food even though he enjoyed cooking it. He watched Shea move back over to the bed, sitting near him. "Aren't you going to eat?" she asked him in concern.

Shaking his head, he said, "I'm not hungry."

"But you need to eat," she insisted, giving him a stern look. "If you don't eat, you'll get sick. And then you won't be able to work here."

That possibility brought him to a blinding halt, and he stared at her in silence. For some reason unbeknownst to him, the idea made him sad. He didn't want to leave. Even though he'd done nothing but make trouble since he'd arrived, he wanted to stay. Kaden carefully picked up the plate and started to slowly eat, eventually enjoying the food. He sighed with satisfaction when he set the plate aside a short time later.

"Good boy." She smiled and ruffled his hair. This amused him since she couldn't be more than a year older than him, if any.

It struck him as she stood and flashed him a grin that she reminded him of his mother. The caring nature, her gentle ways, and her soothing aura were all reminiscent of his mother. He brushed a lock of his dark hair back from his face and watched her as she walked toward the door. "Good night, Kaden. See you in the morning. And don't forget our date on Friday night." She tossed him a wink before leaving the room.

26

Lost in thought for a while, Kaden looked at the clock and saw it was almost ten, and he hadn't done the dishes from dinner yet. He shot up from the bed as if stung and grabbed his plate and glass from the nightstand before darting down the hallway to the kitchen. Amazement brought him to an abrupt stop. The dishes had already been washed, dried, and put away. Chagrin washed over him as he realized that Logan must have done the dishes, and after a long hard day out on the ranch. Damn. When would he learn not to screw something up? Sighing, he approached the sink and washed his own dishes, drying them before putting them away. He wiped down the dining room table and turned to go back to his room when the door leading into the dining room opened.

Logan sighed wearily, running a hand over his face as he entered through the back of the house. It had been a long day, and he needed to be up early, but it looked as if it was going to be an equally long night too. His favorite mare was in labor, which meant that he needed to sit up with the animal until she gave birth. He looked up and saw Kaden standing by the hallway. "Kaden, what are you still doing up? You should be asleep," he admonished tiredly, making his way over to where the phone hung on the wall.

"I came out to do the dishes. But they were already done," Kaden accused guiltily.

The large man brushed it off with a wave of his hand as he picked up the phone and dialed a number by heart. "Hey, Doc. It's Logan Michaels. Sorry to rouse you so late, but Golden Star is going into labor. I need you here."

After a few short questions, the vet disconnected the call, and Logan hung up. "Go to bed, Kaden. I'm going to be up for some time. One of our horses is going into labor, and it appears that it might be a difficult one."

Kaden studied Logan's face and saw the exhaustion that covered it. To his surprise, his heart jolted. Shaking his head as if to clear it, he watched as Logan turned and headed back outside.

Golden Star had been Logan's since he was sixteen. Twelve years ago, his father had bought her for him, and it was one of the few connections he had left to his parents. He entered the barn and began preparing for the long night, settling down inside the stall with his back against the wall. The vet would be there soon.

Deciding to help, since he barely slept anyway because of the nightmares that plagued him, Kaden made a pot of coffee and found one of the travel canisters to pour it into. The night felt cool as he stepped outside, and he could hear the crickets chirping as his sneakers crunched along the ground toward the barn. There were little lights darting around him, and he studied them curiously. He'd never been out of the city, so everything here seemed strange and new to him. A light breeze misted across the field grasses, brushing over his skin and ruffling his hair slightly, bringing with it a strong scent of honeysuckle. He breathed deeply, taking in all of the smells at once, which caused him to sneeze from the overpowering surge on his senses. He caught a glimpse of the white horse from that morning restlessly pacing in its corral.

The barn door squeaked slightly as he opened it, hesitantly stepping inside. His nose wrinkled slightly at the smells of horse flesh, fresh straw, and wood. Several stalls lined each side of the barn, and all of the stalls were occupied right now because of the roundup. Horses of every color were sleeping or eating: black, brown, white, white and brown, white and black. He looked around in awe. The sound of hay rustling drew his attention to one stall that was lit up with a lantern, and he carefully made his way there, gazing inside at a huge black horse. The one that he'd seen in the picture with Logan now lay among the straw. Her body shimmered with sweat, and she lay with her legs curled beneath her, the skin trembling just slightly to show she was in pain. "Kaden?" He heard that smooth-as-melted-chocolate voice and shuddered at the sudden heat that invaded his body.

"I… I thought you might want some coffee." He held out the canister, not stepping into the stall.

Logan beckoned him to enter, but he shook his head, eyeing the horse. The large man released a small laugh and stood, moving over to the stall door and opening it. "Come on. She's not going to hurt you. In fact, she's one of the gentlest horses I've ever had. Her name's Golden Star." It pleased Logan to see the kid have enough trust in him to come in the stall, albeit reluctantly.

"She's beautiful," Kaden commented quietly, taking in the dark black coat, the white marking on her forehead, and the back two feet with white around the hooves. "Is she going to be all right?"

Logan gratefully took the canister, pouring himself a cup before capping it and setting it beside his original sitting place. "She's in labor. I agreed to breed her with a neighbor's horse so that their daughter could have the foal. But I'm almost regretting it because it looks as though it's going to be a hard labor on her."

"Oh." Kaden stayed close to the wall, just observing.

"You should get some sleep. You have to be up early in the morning," Logan commented, carefully watching the boy and the curiosity that covered his features. His breath caught slightly in his throat as the boy looked up at him, and for the first time since his arrival had enough courage to speak back to him with a glare.

"So do you! And… I never sleep much anyway," Kaden stammered slightly, a very becoming blush spreading across his cheeks. What had come over him to speak like that? And to his employer, no less! He mentally sighed because it seemed like he would wind up getting fired and shipped back to New York in no time if he kept it up.

"Too many bad dreams?" Logan probed lightly, and he almost sighed with frustration as the boy tensed before giving a jerky nod. "Yeah. I know all about bad dreams. Well, she should be all right for a while, hopefully until the Doc can get here. Thanks for the coffee."

Kaden didn't want to leave. He wanted to stay and watch but… should he ask? "Can… can I stay and help?" he requested hesitantly, his eyes still trained on the horse breathing heavily.

Logan saw the kid preparing himself for rejection, and there was no way he could tell him to go so he gave in. "It's all right by me. What do you think, Golden Star?" He looked toward the horse, and she let out a weak whicker.

Happiness spread through Kaden, and he sat down where he stood, with his back leaning into the wall, but still several feet from Logan. The horse shifted slightly, crunching some of the hay beneath her heavy weight. He glanced over at Logan, who'd once again relaxed against the wall behind him. The man's eyes were trained on the horse as if waiting for some mysterious sign. He could sense the cowboy was concerned about the horse, and he decided to ask questions to distract Logan from his worry. "How old is she?"

Unable to suppress his surprise at Kaden initiating a conversation, Logan turned his head toward him. It seemed the teenager was starting to feel more comfortable around him, and pleasure spread through him. "She's twelve years old. My father gave her to me when I turned sixteen."

Kaden did quick calculations in his head and found that meant Logan was twenty-eight. Nine years older than himself. "She's very pretty. I saw her picture."

"She's the gentlest horse anyone could ever meet. Unlike Mantacor, outside in the corral. Whatever you do, don't go near him. He'd likely bite you as soon as look at you." Logan tossed his hand in the general direction of the horse he was referring to, and Kaden jolted, shocked. The man was talking about the white horse outside. The one that he'd almost seemed to connect with. But if the horse was as mean and ornery as the man said, why had it let him touch it?

"What's wrong with him?" he questioned quietly, oddly drawn to the horse more than he had been that morning. The thought that he was an outsider like him, or perhaps he'd been through a lot in his past like him, made him long to be with the animal.

"I got him at an auction cheap. He was wild as can be, bucking, biting, and trying to get away from the men holdin' him. If I hadn't bought him, they'd have destroyed him. Much as I'd like to ride him, he won't let me near him. There are scars on his body that indicate abuse and with the crazy look he gets in those eyes, it cements that theory in my mind." The taller man's voice dipped and raised, his tone depending on his emotions as he spoke. It fascinated Kaden to see him so passionate about the creature outside, even though he deemed it mean. Maybe he could... but Kaden cut that line of thought off immediately, berating himself for being so idiotic.

The horse outside reminded Logan of the boy seated nearby. They were two of a kind, those two. A sound brought his head up, and he stood up quickly, startling Kaden, who immediately moved several more feet away. Logan chastised himself for moving so quickly around him before opening the stall door and heading out to meet the vet. "Hey, Doc. How goes it?"

A beautiful red-headed woman stood there, a weary look on her face. Dr. Jessie Riggs was several inches taller than Kaden, with long red hair she currently had braided and twisted up in a loop and amber eyes. Freckles dusted her nose and high cheekbones. "Logan Michaels, this had better be good since you're getting me out of bed this late at night. I just got done with Hanson's mare two hours ago. Colic."

Logan grimaced at that word. Colic could kill a horse if left untreated or if it wasn't treated soon enough. "I think she's in trouble, Doc."

She followed him to the stall, stepping inside and quickly making her way over to the horse. She didn't even notice Kaden where he sat huddled against the side of the stall just watching her movements. Awe and wonder filled his expression as he watched her work. The proficiency in her motions but the gentleness of her hands made him wish he was the horse. His eyes filled with longing to be touched like that. "You're right, Logan. The foal is turned. If we don't get it turned back the right way we'll lose both of them."

Kaden winced when he heard the big man swear profusely and loudly but continued to watch as the doctor and Logan started to do something to the horse. They urged her to her side and began to mess with her rear end. That made Kaden sit up straighter, and he watched the doctor actually start to put her hands inside the horse. "Do... doesn't that hurt her?" he asked frantically, his eyes wide and his heart pounding in distress for the horse.

Logan had all but forgotten the kid, and the doctor hadn't noticed him from the beginning. She glanced at the boy with an arched brow before returning to her task. "It has to be done. Or else they'll both die. One moment of pain to repair the damage is better than hours of torturous pain and then death, Kaden." He explained all of this as patiently as possible, stroking Golden Star's neck.

Kaden inched closer, cautiously reaching out a hand to lightly touch the horse's muzzle. It felt soft underneath his fingers, and he started to tenderly stroke the side of her head, still intently watching the doctor and Logan. Wanting to soothe the horse and take away some of her pain, he leaned down and began to softly croon into her ear. A song long forgotten, long buried away with all of his memories, rose to the surface. His mother had sung it to him as a child as she tucked him into bed. The horse seemed to calm and let out a soft snort, her eyes closing. It felt like something compelled him to comfort the horse, to help her get through her pain. Like no one had ever helped him.

Amazement traveled through Logan as he watched and listened to the young man. He couldn't hear the words, but it had an astonishing effect on the horse, and he felt the horse's muscles relax slightly. Even Doc Riggs couldn't hide her awe at the way Kaden affected the horse. She quickly finished turning the foal, making sure that it came out forelegs first.

When the vet was done, Kaden continued to caress the horse and sing into her ear. Golden Star lifted her head several times to look back at what was happening, but he ignored everything except the animal. Finally, Logan gently touched his shoulder to get his attention. Kaden almost leaped out of his skin at the touch and swung his head around, his eyes haunted.

Logan felt disappointed that he still seemed afraid of him, but he supposed it was natural considering he'd only known him two days. "It's time for her to do her own thing," he explained slowly, pointing out the fact that the foal had been born and the mother needed to clean it and start to nurse.

Kaden stepped back, dangerously close to Logan's side without realizing it, and watched as Golden Star struggled to stand and then proceeded to clean the foal. "It's a baby girl," the larger man said.

The foal was beautiful. Inky black like the mother but the two forelegs had white socks, and instead of a simple star on her forehead, she had a huge blaze of white down her muzzle. The foal slowly stood to its legs, gangly and unused, falling several times before it managed to stay up. Kaden smiled as the foal nudged toward its mother and began to nurse. He felt a curious wetness on his cheeks and lifted his hand to touch them. He was crying! It shocked him to find that he could still cry, and happy tears at that. "Come on, let's get some rest," Logan said gruffly, glad to have shared the moment with the boy.

Doc Riggs said goodnight and left, heading home to her warm bed. Kaden waited at the entrance of the barn for Logan. Logan followed not long after and smiled tiredly. "You did good, kid. Thank you for your help tonight."

"I didn't do anything," Kaden protested, his eyes wide with surprise that the man would think he did anything.

"Of course you did. You were my moral support. And you helped Golden Star, which I'm sure she's grateful for and would tell you if she could," Logan pointed out, gazing down at the boy in the moonlight. He wanted to reach out and touch the soft skin of his cheek, to brush that annoying lock of hair that always clung to his face back, and to lean down and ravish those upturned, inviting lips. That thought brought him to an abrupt, horrified halt. What the hell was he thinking? Kissing another man?

Kaden gazed up at Logan, unaware of the turmoil behind the man's eyes. "I just felt the need to help her. To lessen her pain in any way I could," he explained in discomfort, moving away from the man, feeling intimidated again.

Lust and desire spread even faster through Logan, and he swallowed hard, shifting as his pants became a little tighter. Thank God for his date on Friday! Maybe he could release a little frustration then. That's all it was, he tried to convince himself. He just hadn't gotten laid in a while, and the boy did look a little feminine. *That's it.* With a brisk mental nod, he smiled broadly at Kaden. "Well, you did help. A lot. What song were you singing?"

Memories of his mother caused his features to soften as Kaden thought of those moments with her. "It was a song my mother used to sing to me as a child when she would put me to bed. It's called 'All Through the Night'."

34

They had reached the front porch by then, and Logan motioned for him to sit on the swing. Kaden hesitated, not sure if he should trust his instincts, screaming at him to run, or his heart, screaming at him to stay. For once, he gave in to his heart and perched uneasily on the edge of the swing, ready to leap up at a moment's notice. Logan casually settled onto the seat beside him, his palms sweating. He rubbed them against his thighs, drying them on his jeans. "Will you sing it for me?" Logan requested in a low tone.

"Oh... no... I... I couldn't," Kaden protested, shaking his head furiously.

"Please?" the larger man urged. "I'd like to hear the song you sang to Golden Star."

He tried to get out of it but Logan wouldn't allow him, and finally he gave into the cowboy's wishes and, in a hushed voice, began to sing the song he'd crooned into Golden Star's ear as she lay in pain. The words were laden with affection, deep with love. They pulled him away from the pain and the uncertainty. On the last, his voice held such sweet emotion that he flushed.

As his voice faded away, he felt Logan's eyes on him, and he was grateful for the darkness that surrounded them because his face felt like it was on fire. He knew his cheeks had to be as bright as a tomato. "That was beautiful," the larger man breathed out, causing Kaden to shift in discomfort.

"Uh... we should really get some sleep since we have to be up in three hours." He stood and made his way to the front door, pulling the screen door open only to stop when Logan called his name. He kept his back to Logan with his hand on the doorknob.

"I just want you to know that even though you've only known me for a couple of days, if you ever need anything, all you need to do is ask," the cowboy stated, his voice low and melodious.

Kaden felt his heart twinge, and his breathing grew shallow. No one had cared about him in a long time, and to hear those words made him even sadder. "Good night, Logan." With that, he entered the house and walked to his room to lie down. Sleep never came, and he was up before the alarm went off.

CHAPTER 4

THE next two days passed uneventfully, for which both men were grateful, and Friday morning dawned bright and sunny. Kaden was regretting his decision to go out with Shea that night to dance, and it was brought to the forefront of his mind when she called cheerily, "I'll see you tonight at seven, Kaden," before heading out the front door. He sighed and continued to wipe down the kitchen counters before moving to the dining room table.

The men were already gone, and he had the entire day stretching before him until seven. He had yet to clean anything upstairs. Actually, he hadn't even been to the upstairs yet. So with a guilty sense of curiosity, he hesitantly took the steps one at a time. The banister was white and went in a straight line down to the first floor. It was a perfect banister for sliding down, and he could almost picture Logan and Shea fighting over who got to do it first. His lips curled into a smile as he saw Logan with his sandy blond hair and bright green eyes whooshing down the wooden banister, letting out a war cry as he went. And of course, Shea, arguing over the fact that she could do it, too, following him down the banister. It made him chuckle as he thought of her insistence at being treated as an equal.

Over the course of the past few days, he'd seen how Logan treated Shea as if she were made of glass and would break any moment. It frustrated her to no end, and she'd even sat with Kaden late one night when he couldn't sleep and talked about how she didn't want to be away from the ranch, but Logan had forced her to go away to college. He wondered if Logan even knew how much Shea wanted to be with him here at the ranch instead of away and worrying about him. Kaden stopped along the stairs to study the pictures that hung on the walls. There was a picture of a kind-looking man and a woman holding one another in wedding attire. They must be Logan and Shea's parents. He had not had the nerve to ask where they were. He studied the picture, and saw Logan's features in their father and Shea's in their mother, except he would bet with a certainty that her stubbornness came from the father because their chins were the same, strong and sturdy.

The next few photographs along the way were pictures of Logan and Shea in various stages of their lives. One showed Logan in high school with a huge smile, holding a football. There was another that was a prom picture of the big, kind cowboy. In it, he was holding a shorter girl with bright red curls against his side, with a wide grin splitting his features. He looked so handsome in a tuxedo, tall and dashing. But Kaden noted the girl in the picture and sighed with resignation. It wasn't like the man would ever be interested in someone like him, someone with mental problems, and unable to do anything physically. So he continued up the stairs, reaching the second-floor landing. There were only four bedrooms upstairs along with a bathroom. The first bedroom must have been a guestroom, as it stood untouched, so he continued on to the next room.

The room was undeniably Shea's. There were Harvard pennants on the walls, a large canopy bed in the middle of the room against the wall, a white bedroom set, a vanity table littered with makeup and perfume, and a window seat that was perfect to look out over the ranch while reading a book. The walls were a light purple color with a border of yellow daisies along the top of the wall. It made him pause briefly and grin. Even though she tried

38

so hard to be thought of as another cowboy, she really was a feminine woman at heart. It didn't appear that the room needed to be cleaned and Kaden backed out of the room, closing the door behind him.

Swallowing with difficulty, his eyes locked on the white door at the end of the hall as he walked slowly toward it. He hesitated for a fraction of a second as he rested his hand on the golden doorknob before twisting it and carefully pushed the door open. The room inside reeked of masculinity. There was no other word for it. A huge king-size oak wood bed rested against the middle of one wall, an oak dresser dominated the other, and there was another rocking chair in the room. Sheesh, this family really had a thing for rocking chairs. The walls were a light coffee color and complimented the smoky gray carpet, leaving the impression that Logan had decorated the room himself. But the thing that struck him the hardest was that the bed remained unmade, there were clothes littering the floor, and a glance into the bathroom made him cringe. Geez, the man was a pig! With a resolute sigh, he started slowly and began to pick up the clothing, finding the hamper in the closet, which appeared to be overflowing as well. So, picking up the hamper, he headed downstairs to the laundry room that was off the kitchen.

It felt odd to be touching the man's things, and his face flamed bright red when he came across Logan's underwear in the hamper. But he resolutely continued separating the clothing. The first load was all jeans. The rest he set aside in piles to continue with later before taking the hamper back upstairs to get the rest of the man's dirty clothes. Kaden kept an eye on the clock because he would need to start lunch soon in order to have it all prepared by the time the men got there. Today they were in the corrals again, branding the new calves they'd brought in from the fields. After ensuring all the clothes were in the laundry room downstairs, he approached the bed. His heartbeat increased as he straightened out the pillows, causing the scent of Logan's shampoo to rise from the soft clouds of fabric. The scent caused a reaction in his lower half, instantly making him hard with arousal. Shock and shame overcame him, and he sank down to his knees, waiting for the sensations to pass. Arousal was something to be ashamed and afraid of. It left you open for pain and embarrassment. Tears stung his eyes, and he clenched his fists against jeans-clad thighs.

It took a few moments but the feeling faded, and he slowly dragged himself up from the floor. Nibbling nervously at his bottom lip, he finished mechanically making the bed, making sure the quilt was straight before going into Logan's bathroom. There was no other word to describe the bathroom except huge. The tiles on the floor were white as were the tiles that went halfway up the walls. The areas that remained untiled were a light yellow. A shower stall was in one corner and needed a cleaning badly. The plexiglass surface was practically opaque with soap scum. A large hot-tub-style bathtub dominated the other corner, and he began to imagine Logan naked and wet in that tub, his broad chest gleaming in the light from above the oversized mirror. His hands shook as he started to clean up the bathroom counter, wiping down the stainless steel faucets and sink, throwing away the used razors that had been carelessly tossed aside.

Kaden opened the medicine chest to start putting away the shaving cream and cologne that sat on the counter, but he froze when his eyes settled on the box of condoms sitting on the bottom shelf of the cabinet. This time his body responded with a vengeance, and he started to hyperventilate, his breathing shallow and quick. Backing away with his eyes still trained on that box, he brought one hand to his other wrist and dug his nails in, trying to stop the anxiety flooding him. He started scratching, digging the nails deeply to try and stem the pain in his heart with the physical pain in his wrist. Reaching out, he slammed the cabinet shut and turned away, leaning his forehead against the shower stall door. Relax, his mind screamed at him. Finally the pain in his wrist grabbed his attention, and he weakly slumped against the shower door. Little drops of blood had fallen to the floor. His fingers were covered in the red liquid, and it was embedded beneath his nails. There would be no way to hide this. He would have to wear the black leather wrist band he had for the next week until it healed. Damn it. Why was he so stupid?

With a resigned and pained sigh, he stepped over to the sink and carefully washed the wounds, watching the pink water swirling down the drain. Then he closed his eyes, opened the medicine chest, and reached to the top shelf, where he'd noticed the package of gauze. It would be the only way to cover it and stop the bleeding. He shut the small door before opening his eyes again and taking out the package of gauze. Kaden carefully wrapped his still-bleeding wrist, watching the red stain the snow-white fabric. It reminded him of that day, the blood splattered across the floor, and the lifeless eyes staring up at him. Growling low in his throat, Kaden roughly rammed those memories deep into his brain, demanding that he forget everything. He didn't want to remember anymore. It only caused more pain. It seemed that was all his life consisted of. Ever since he'd been a child, the only thing he had experienced was pain, in one form or another.

Once the bandage was in place, he cleaned up the evidence of his wounds and took everything down to throw away in the garbage in the kitchen where Logan or Shea wouldn't see. Then he quickly grabbed the leather wrist band from his room and snapped it into place, making sure none of the gauze showed outside of the covering. He had to start preparing lunch or he'd never finish in time, and he began to fix three heaping pans of homemade chicken pot pie. He spread pie crusts along the bottom and sides of the pans, making sure it all was covered. Then he began to cut up the chicken he'd cooked the night before and left in the fridge, spreading it along the bottom of the pie crust before adding cans of pre-cut potato pieces, corn, peas, and carrots. Then he added in several huge jars of chicken gravy, mixing it directly in the pan before covering it with the remaining pie crusts. To add a spice of flavor to the pie crusts, he sprinkled fresh grated parmesan cheese along the tops before putting them in the already preheated oven.

The pot pies would only take an hour and a half to cook which left him enough time to make up large pitchers of iced tea and lemonade for their drinks. Everything was ready and waiting for the men when they arrived, and he could hear them entering the dining room, exclaiming over the food and drinks. It had become a routine with them. Every time they entered the room they made a big deal about complimenting the food and expressing their enjoyment. Logan had talked about the men wanting to meet him, and he'd immediately become paralyzed with fear. Being in a room full of big, strong, brash men was the depths of hell for him, and there was no way he would be able to stand it without experiencing a panic attack. He would make excuses, disappearing before he could be talked into it.

Before heading into his bedroom, he grabbed a glass of iced tea and a small plate of the chicken pot pie he'd set aside for himself. He'd been eating regularly the last two days, and the dizziness he usually felt had faded away. It had been a while since he'd felt any. So he continued to eat. Surprisingly, even after that morning's panic attack, he still felt hungry. He set the plate on his nightstand and pulled out the lyric book, sighing with disappointment when he saw how close he was to running out of room in the book. He wondered if Logan would mind if Charlie picked one up for him when he went into town to get supplies. He'd made up a list yesterday of all the groceries he needed and had meant to give it to Charlie that day so that the older man could go into town, but he'd forgotten. Maybe he could offer money for the book, and then it wouldn't be that bad. Besides, being on the ranch all the time, he didn't have anywhere to spend the money so he would have the entire salary saved by the time he went back to New York City.

He'd been on the ranch now for almost a full five days, and

even though he'd had panic attacks and made mistakes, they hadn't tried to hurt him or yelled at him. They'd only encouraged him, and it confused him. Why would someone be okay with him making a mistake? Mistakes weren't all right. They were bad. They could cause worse mistakes to happen. Or they could cause bigger problems for the people around him. He'd gotten his confusion out in his lyrics. The songs he'd written the last few days were so different from the ones he'd written in the past, and he'd read them again and again, seeing the difference. Looking around the large room, he wondered if he'd be ready to go back to New York City at the end of the three months. After being here only a short time, it would seem so barren and foreign when he returned. He didn't know if he wanted to go back, but he'd have no choice. Where else could he go? He had no one else but himself.

A knock sounded at his door, and Kaden set his notebook aside and hefted himself from the bed. He was surprised to find Charlie standing there. "Hey, Charlie." He smiled happily.

"I was wondering about that list. For the supplies," Charlie explained. "I wanted to head into town really soon because tonight's my night off, and I have some plans." A fine flush spread up the man's neck and across his cheeks.

"Oh. Of course." Kaden walked over to his nightstand and opened the drawer there to take out the list he'd made. He hesitated for a brief second before grabbing his pen and adding the notation about the composition book. He picked up his book to bring over to Charlie to show him what he wanted. "I… uh… was kind of hoping you could buy me another one of these books while you're there." He showed the little man the book. "I can give you money." Charlie waved away his offer of money.

"Why don't you come with me? That way you can pick out what you want," Charlie said with a smile.

"Oh, I don't know if I should. I have to be back to fix dinner and all."

"We'll be back in time. We'll only be gone about an hour or so. Logan won't mind. In fact, I'll just let him know when we leave." The little man turned without another word, clearly expecting Kaden to follow, which he did reluctantly after putting his notebook away and grabbing his wallet. He didn't have much money in there, but he had enough to afford the book he wanted.

Charlie had already spoken to Logan by the time Kaden met him out front, and he climbed into the same truck from the other day with the man. "So what do you write in that little book of yours?" Charlie asked as they drove toward town.

Kaden wasn't sure he wanted to share in case the man asked to see it or told someone else. "It's... just... uh... stuff that wanders around in my head."

"Oh, like a journal or something? That's a good way to get stress out too. I used to have one of those when I was around your age. 'Course, it's long gone by now. So how do you find the job so far? I have to tell you, the men love your cooking. And today's lunch, I haven't eaten something that good since I can remember." The man let out a sound of appreciation.

"It's really nice here. And the job is easy. I like it. I'm glad to know everyone likes the food," he replied, nervously shifting around on the seat.

"And that Franklin. All he can do is talk about you. He says that if you were a woman, he'd kidnap you and force you to marry him just for your cooking." Charlie had no way of knowing that Kaden detested that man and how much being told that would terrify him, but Kaden almost let out a small cry of fear at the thought. There was no way he would marry a slimy weasel like that one even if he were female.

A few moments later, they reached the nearby town. It wasn't the same as the city his plane had landed in, and he looked around curiously. There were small stores of all kinds: a beauty salon, a hardware store, a feed store for ranchers and farmers, a grocery store, and several other side places, even an antique store. When Charlie pulled up in front of the grocery store, Kaden stepped out slowly, cautious about strangers. "Come on." Charlie beckoned for him to follow him into the store.

It was a good-size grocery store, not a mom-and-pop joint like he'd expected, and he followed Charlie around as the man grabbed the groceries on the list, adding huge amounts of each item. "The school supply aisle is about four aisles that way. Why don't you head on over and grab your notebook," the older man said, glancing around nervously at him.

His brow furrowed, Kaden nodded and headed the way the man had pointed, finding the aisle with ease and wandering down it. The composition books were on the bottom rack, and not knowing if he'd get back to town again in the next few months, he grabbed two and moved off to find Charlie. The man stood at the deli counter, and Kaden could see an older woman about his age standing behind the counter. It appeared as though they were flirting with each other. That made him stop in his tracks, and he watched the way the little man shifted from foot to foot. It made Kaden smile to see such a display from a man that age. Deciding to give them time to themselves, he wandered around just studying the various types of foods and drinks in the store. It always amazed him to see how many types and styles of food there were in the world. He stopped at the meat area and looked over the selection, pausing when he came to something labeled calf fries. Calf fries? What the hell was that?

"Hey, Kaden! Did you find what you needed?" Charlie asked as he stepped up beside him with two heaping baskets of groceries.

Kaden nodded and then pointed at the item. "What are those?"

"Calf fries? Oh, those are the most delicious when you fry them up with butter, oil, and garlic. Or put them on the grill outside." The man made a smacking sound with his lips. That still didn't explain what they were specifically, so Kaden turned and looked at Charlie with a questioning look. That caused the man to stutter a little. "Well… uh… th-they're uh…." He leaned forward and whispered into Kaden's ear, causing the kid to rear back in horror.

"They're what?" Kaden practically shouted, his voice high with disgust.

"You heard me," Charlie mumbled, and he looked around to see a couple of neighbors looking at them curiously. He smiled tightly and nodded at them before turning back to the teenager. "You all right, Kaden? You look a little green around the gills, there."

"That's…." He stopped. People actually ate cow testicles? What the hell was wrong with them? A shudder of disgust and horror ran down his spine. "Did you get everything on the list?" He turned his back on the calf fries.

"Yeah. You ready to go?" Charlie asked.

The kid nodded and walked with the man back to the front after taking over one of the carts. They started putting everything on the counter for the cashier to ring up. The woman kept glancing at Kaden curiously, causing him to feel slightly uncomfortable. Her name tag said Doris. She had way too much makeup on too. She finally asked the question that had been burning on the tip of her tongue. "Are you the new cook up on Logan's spread?"

Instead of responding verbally, he just tipped his head yes.

"Young one, ain't ya? And a man, to boot. That's a surprise. Usually he likes his cooks young, pretty, and female. He don't get out much, if you know what I mean," the woman drawled.

"Leave the kid alone, Doris," Charlie snapped. "And get back to work. Don't mind her, son. She's just jealous because he won't look at an old hag like her."

She glared at the little man and popped her gum, finishing up the rest of the groceries angrily. Kaden almost dropped to the ground when he heard the amount she said. He hadn't seen that much money spent on food in his entire lifetime. When Charlie saw the composition books still in his hand, he reached out and snatched them from him. "These too."

Kaden tried to protest, but Charlie just gave him a look and watched as Doris rang them up. They loaded everything into the truck and were on their way back to the ranch in minutes. Charlie soothed him on the way home. "Don't worry too much about it, Kaden. You deserve it after all the hard work you've put in. And besides, it's not like they were a hundred dollars or anything. Fifty cents each. A dollar ain't goin' ta break the bank, if ya know what I mean."

So he finally relented and breathed a sigh of relief when the ranch came back into view. Now he just had to get all the groceries put away and fix dinner. Trepidation filled him as the time inched closer and closer to seven and his date with Shea. He didn't view her in any other way than sisterly, so he hoped she didn't intend it to be a true date. Besides, he didn't have a whole lot of money on him. Maybe he should explain that before going.

They quickly unloaded the truck, and Kaden started unpacking everything. He made several trips down to the basement to store the meats in the large chest freezer. Finally, all the food put away, he started dinner, and it was on the table steaming hot by the time the men arrived. Shea was moments behind them, and she came into the kitchen immediately. "Hey, Kaden. Ready for our date tonight?" She winked at him and sat at the small table in there to eat.

He wanted so badly to go back to his room, but she'd come in there to keep him company so he settled down to eat with her. "Shea... I, um... I don't really have a whole lot of money... uh...."

She stopped him with a heated look. "I didn't ask you to go dancing expecting you to pay for me, Kaden. I just wanted to go out and have fun. And I want you to go with me. So you can wipe that look off your face, because this isn't a real date." She shoved a forkful of food into her mouth and chewed angrily.

He flushed and looked down at his plate, his appetite gone. "I didn't mean to offend you. I just didn't know if you were expecting that or not."

The girl's face softened, and she reached out to place her hand on his. "It's all right. I understand. I didn't exactly explain it as I should have. I'll treat you to a drink tonight. Of course, since you're not twenty-one, it'll be non-alcoholic."

"I wouldn't drink alcohol anyway," Kaden said tersely, standing up to empty his plate and wash it in the sink. He could feel the curiosity rolling off her in waves, but ignored it. He just hoped tonight wouldn't be another mistake on his part. He wasn't sure if he shouldn't just back out of it, but Shea was humming happily as she ate, and he couldn't disappoint her, especially after how nice she had been to him. So with a resigned mindset he went to get dressed in the only outfit he had that wasn't torn, faded jeans and T-shirts.

CHAPTER 5

THE outfit consisted of black leather pants and a black T-shirt that he kept for any reason he might need to look slightly less casual. But still, it went well with his pale skin, the black leather wrist band, and his violet eyes. Staring in the mirror, he wondered for the millionth time why he was doing this. Not only would he not fit in, he didn't even know if he would be able to dance with Shea. After brushing his hair back from his face and making sure his boots were tied tightly, Kaden wandered back down to the kitchen and found Shea waiting for him. He stared at her. She'd let her hair loose from the braid, and it hung around her shoulders and back, a cascade of golden curls. She was wearing a blue-jean skirt with a red tank top and a white button-down shirt that she'd tied loosely into a knot at her waist. On her feet were black boots that ended mid-calf. He suddenly felt a little oddly dressed and looked from his clothes to hers and back again.

"You look great, Kaden," she squealed, coming forward to grab his hand and tug him toward the front door. "Come on. Logan's still upstairs getting ready for his own date. Let's go."

"But I need to tell him that I—" She cut him off with a look and kept a tight grip on his hand to drag him out the front door.

Kaden sighed, giving in to the insistent girl before him. She led him to her blue compact Toyota Corolla, unlocking his door before going around to the driver's side. "This is going to be great," Shea said excitedly as she started up the car. "I'll teach you the moves. I think you'll have a lot of fun, Kaden. I really do. I promise."

"I still don't know about this, Shea," he said quietly, gazing out the window at the dark countryside whizzing by.

"Oh, will you please give it a chance? If you really aren't comfortable, just tell me, and we'll come back," Shea said, compromising with him.

So he again gave in to her, and about fifteen minutes later they pulled up in front of a western saloon-style place. He stared at the wooden building before him with its neon signs advertising beers, and another one proclaiming the best honky-tonk in the country. He still didn't know what that was. Shea leaped from the car, and he slowly climbed out, meeting her in front. She took his hand again and led him toward the door. He could hear country music blasting from the building before they even stepped inside, and when the door opened, he winced at the loud music beating at his eardrums. A smoky haze permeated the air of the bar, and a live band stood up on the stage, with a crowd of people milling around on the dance floor. Tables were occupied by various people: groups of men, couples, and even just groups of women. The barstools were mostly taken up by single men and women looking for a good time.

Kaden heard several loud voices calling out greetings to Shea, and even a catcall. She just grinned and waved or shouted back. One man stepped away from the bar and strode toward them. Kaden's eyes widened as he watched the man approach, and he felt her hand squeeze his reassuringly. He forced himself to relax, his eyes warily trained on the newcomer.

"Shea Michaels?" The man's voice was deep and held an incredulous tone. "Well, would you look at what the cat drug in?

All grown up, ain't ya? I thought you'd still be off at that fancy school o' yours." He was a good-looking guy by today's standards: tall, muscular, and tanned, with a head of thick brown hair and light blue eyes.

"Ty Coolson, you back off of that young lady now!" a baritone voice shouted from behind the bar.

Ty glared at the man who'd shouted before turning back to Shea. Kaden saw the way his eyes traveled up and down Shea's body, and the flare of desire for his friend. He glared up at the taller guy, tugging her around him and toward the dance floor. "Kaden!" she exclaimed in surprise at his rudeness.

"You wanted to dance so teach me," he demanded.

Shea stared at him for a split second, thinking that maybe he was jealous, before shrugging it off. The next song started, and she began to show him the line-dancing steps to that song, following along with the crowd around them. Kaden picked it up easily and before long actually began laughing with her. Shea was amazed at the sound of his delightful, musical laughter. It made him seem so young, and it was the first time she had heard him laugh since he'd come to the ranch. His eyes lost the haunted look that she'd seen since she'd met him, and he seemed to shed his fears. When a slow song came on he wanted to go grab a drink and sit down, but she took his hand and placed it on her waist, then picked up his other hand. "Come on, Kaden. I like slow dancing. It's the best part." She winked at him and grinned broadly when he flushed.

Kaden felt the tiny waist beneath his fingers and knew that he had started to actually care for the girl. He would do whatever it took to protect her. He almost choked when she laid her head on his shoulder as they danced. He could feel his cheeks becoming flushed with embarrassment because he could see people watching them, including the man from earlier. But his expression showed annoyance and jealousy instead of indulgence or curiosity. Kaden smirked at the man and spun her around, causing her to laugh at his

51

antics. Maybe taunting the stranger hadn't been the best thing to do, because the man stood up and strode toward the floor. Kaden immediately shrank back, the smile fading.

Shea noticed his stiffening and turned her head to see Ty heading their way. With a roll of her eyes, she turned back to Kaden and caught the look of fear in his eyes. Dammit. And they had been having so much fun. Letting go of Kaden's hand, she turned around to look at Ty. "Not now, Ty. Go away," she demanded.

Ty stepped forward, his hands clenched at his sides. "Damn it, Shea. You go away and come back for the summer with some fruitcake boy from Harvard, and you expect me to just stand by to watch him steal you away from me?"

Shock came over Kaden, and he stared at them as though they'd suddenly started tap dancing. His gaze shifted between the two of them as they talked. "Ty, I did not come back from Harvard with some 'fruitcake' boy as you put it! He's working for my brother, and I brought him out as a *friend.*" She stressed that word to make sure the man understood. "He hasn't been off the ranch since he got here. Now back off!" She had started shouting by the time she finished, and Kaden could feel the anger rolling off of her.

"Shea," he said hesitantly, trying to get her attention. He still felt uneasy, and it grew the longer they stood there. More people were staring at the spectacle they were making. "Maybe you should dance with him? I'll just go sit at the bar and have a Coke."

Shea looked at him and saw his exhaustion, giving in with a sigh and a nod. "All right. But don't leave the bar, okay?"

Kaden nodded and headed that way, finding an empty stool to perch on. He ordered a Coke and watched Shea start dancing with the bigger man, still locked in a heated conversation. "Don't worry none about Shea," the bartender shouted over the music as he placed the soda in front of Kaden. "Everyone in this town knows her. No one could lay a hand on her without the entire town knowing. Ty was just jealous is all. I'm Vic."

"Kaden," he shouted back, his eyes still on Shea.

"You working up at the Michaels's place?" the bartender asked curiously, studying the fragile boy before him.

He nodded while taking a sip of the soda. "I'm cooking for the roundup," he explained.

"Where you from?"

"New York."

"City? I bet you find this place completely different from what you're used to." The bartender became distracted for a second and looked up. "Oh, looks like it's a family thing tonight!"

Kaden swiveled on the stool to find Logan stepping just inside the door with a pretty woman at his side. His heart twisted, and his stomach clenched. Sweat popped out on his forehead, and he swung back to face the bar, his fingers unconsciously tightening on the glass. He tried to ignore the fact that he knew Logan was there, but the man in question stepped up to the bar beside him to order a beer.

"Kaden? What are you doing here?" Logan stepped closer to be heard over the music, and Kaden tried to keep from pulling away.

"Shea brought me." He pointed at the girl on the dance floor.

Logan shook his head when he saw who Shea was with, and a dark expression dominated his face. He swore beneath his breath and would have started over to the dance floor, but the woman stopped him. She said something to him, and he seemed to relax. Petite and soft, she had dark brown hair that hung in ringlets down to the middle of her back and sterling silver eyes that shone intelligently in the dim lights. He could see why Logan would like her. She was beautiful, with flawless porcelain skin, probably silky to the touch, and bright red lips that begged to be kissed. Kaden looked down into his soda, depression settling over him. Standing up, Kaden asked the bartender for the bathroom and headed that way. He needed a few moments away from everything.

Mostly empty, there were only two other guys going about their business in the restroom when he stepped up to the sink, staring at himself in the mirror. His eyes were dark with pain and dark smudges underlined them, making them seem an even deeper hue. To keep from drawing attention, he pretended to wash his hands while trying to get his mind back in order.

"Kaden James? Well I certainly didn't expect to find you in a place like this."

Kaden shuddered with fear and disgust as that voice caressed his skin. He lifted his head to meet those rat-like eyes in the mirror.

"I'm not staying long," he replied warily, watching the way the man seemed to strip him bare with his gaze.

"You're not leaving before I get a dance out of ya." Franklin grabbed his hand, causing Kaden to try and pull away. Anger flared in those brown eyes, and Franklin wouldn't let go, tightening his grip painfully. Kaden bit his lip to keep from whimpering as Franklin practically dragged him out of the bathroom and onto the dance floor. The man yanked him into his arms and up against his body.

Kaden struggled to get away. He felt sheer terror pounding inside him. His heart raced as he became paralyzed with fear. Helplessness invaded him, and his body went limp. Franklin noticed that the boy seemed to lose all the fight in his body and tugged him closer, grinding his stiffening erection against him. The man's lips pressed against his ear and he whispered, "That's it, baby. I can show you a good time. You just need to relax, is all. You are so hot. I almost can't wait to be buried deep inside that body of yours."

Tears flooded Kaden's eyes. He didn't understand why men treated him the way they did. Something seemed to snap inside him and, in a fit of rage, he brought his knee up and rammed it into Franklin's groin, causing the man to groan in pain and drop to the floor, clutching his privates. Blindly tearing through the crowd of people, he didn't hear the brother and sister call his name or notice when Logan headed toward the man lying on the floor. The only thing he knew was that he had to get away from there. The door banged against the wall as he sprinted through it. He rushed toward Shea's car and frantically tugged on the handles to get inside. It was locked, and he pounded weakly on the window. He leaned his head against the cool metal as tears dripped on the smooth surface, running down the glass like raindrops.

"Kaden?" He heard Shea's voice behind him, and then he felt her gentle hand on his back, rubbing it soothingly.

He collapsed to the ground, his hands fisting in the dirt beneath him. Sobs wracked his body as he cried. Shea gathered him close to her, the softness of her body pressing against the sharp angles of his. The scent of her natural perfume and flowery shampoo drifted over him. It reminded him so much of his mother. He buried his face in her neck and just let out his emotions. She whispered soothing words to him, rubbing his back and rocking him. "If you keep this up you'll make yourself sick, Kaden. Please stop crying."

Logan stood there, his knuckles bruised and aching, and his stomach clenching at the shattered cries coming from the boy in his sister's arms. His eyes met hers, and they shared a look of utter helplessness. How did you stop a heart from breaking? How can you change someone's past? Murderous rage raced through Logan's veins, and he closed his eyes, sending a prayer heavenward. He'd fired Franklin right after he'd punched the man and warned the bastard to stay away from the kid.

"Kaden," he called quietly, stiffening when he saw how Kaden trembled and pressed even closer to Shea. "Let's go home, okay?" He stepped closer, squatting close to his sister and the boy.

He reached out and gently placed a hand on Kaden's shoulder, almost crying as well when the teenager seemed to shrink even further into himself. He started to rub his shoulder and remembered the night that Golden Star had her foal. The words that Kaden had sung to him afterward came to mind, and he started to sing softly. His voice low and calm as the words flowed from his lips. He almost smiled with relief and joy when he felt the boy start to relax. The tension eased from Kaden's body, leaving him limp and weak against Shea. Shea gave Logan a questioning look, but he just shook his head and continued to sing Kaden's song.

Kaden heard Logan's voice from a long way off. He was singing his mother's song! The voice was smooth and low, calming his emotions and bringing him back from the edge he'd been on. That awful man's actions had triggered the memories of things he wished he could forget. The oily skin pressing against his, the hard length digging into his stomach, and the scent of sweat and alcohol on the man had gagged him. But now Logan crouched beside him, his hand tenderly caressing his back and his voice crooning to him, calling to him. Everything called Kaden back to him. His tears slowed and his sobs began to quiet, drifting off to nothing but hiccuping sighs. The song faded away, and he lay there, exhausted. Embarrassment came fast on the heels of his panic attack, and he couldn't face them as he pulled away from the girl. "I'm sorry," he whispered ashamedly.

"There's nothing to be sorry for," Shea said fiercely. "That bastard forced himself on you, and had no right to touch you when you so obviously didn't want it. I'd have killed him myself if Logan hadn't already beat him up."

Kaden jerked in surprise and brought his head around to look at Logan. His eyes were wide with wonder as he stared at the larger man, who was still squatting beside them. The man gave him a sheepish look and reached up to rub the back of his own neck. "The bastard deserved it!" Logan exclaimed, his eyes shifting toward the ground and away from the gaze locked on him.

"Thank you," Kaden said, his expression one of gratefulness.

"You're welcome. I just wish I had noticed sooner," Logan replied his voice filled with guilt.

Baffled, Kaden protested, "It's not your fault. I shouldn't have left the bar like Shea told me."

"You shouldn't have to worry about a man like him," the cowboy growled. "He was warned to stay away from you. Well, he won't get another chance because I fired him."

"Eh? But… but… why?" Kaden panicked at the thought that he might have caused too much trouble.

"Because he went against my orders and touched you." Logan spoke without thinking and then realized how that sounded. "I, uh…."

For the first time since they'd met, Kaden initiated contact between them and reached out to touch the older man's cheek. "Thank you," he whispered, his fingers flexing slightly against the hard cheek beneath them before he pulled away.

Logan wanted nothing more than to snatch Kaden's hand and bring it back to his face, but he shoved the urge away. Not only would that not be appropriate, it would probably frighten the kid again. It humbled him that Kaden felt comfortable enough with him to touch him like that. "Come on, let's go. I think we all need some rest."

Kaden carefully stood, his legs somewhat shaky, and helped Shea to her feet. His eyes were red-rimmed, and dirt streaked his clothes. He brushed off as much as he could before climbing into the passenger seat beside Shea. Logan walked back inside to tell his date good night and back out to his own truck. Logan followed behind Shea and Kaden, making sure that they got home all right.

Kaden was on his way to his room when Logan called his name. He tensed, wondering if this was where he finally got fired. He made a mental decision that if that was the case then he would go with as much dignity and as little trouble as possible, so he swung around to face Logan standing in the doorway of the kitchen.

"I know that we've only just met and that you don't trust me just yet." Kaden went to protest that statement but Logan cut him off with a wry smile and a look. "I know you don't trust me. And I understand that. But when you're ready to talk, and you need someone to talk to, I'm here for you. Always."

Kaden's breathing deepened at the implication behind Logan's words, but his own voice seemed lost to him. He didn't know if he would ever be ready to reveal his past to Logan. But he gave a small nod and a smile to show he understood before continuing on to his bedroom. He was already beginning to trust the older man, even though his brain was screaming at him not to. For some reason, he felt a tiny bit of his heart opening to the man, and wondered if it would be another mistake on his part. He stripped his clothes off, tossing them into the trash can. There was no way he could wear those again without remembering that slimy man's hands all over him. After dressing in a pair of sweatpants and a T-shirt, the urge to retreat to a place he felt safe overwhelmed him. He grabbed his notebook and the small flashlight in his nightstand drawer before going into the closet and shutting the door. It was a childish action, he knew that, but he'd never been able to beat it. It was the only place he felt he was able to hide.

CHAPTER 6

ONCE his nerves had calmed, his hands had stopped shaking, and he was successfully able to lock his memories away, Kaden exited the closet and sank down on the edge of the bed, the book open beside him. It was almost time for him to get up for preparing the breakfast meal, so he didn't bother trying to lie down and sleep. Instead, he went to his duffel bag and dug through it to find his cigarettes and lighter. He didn't smoke a whole lot, but whenever he had the urge he gave in. Carefully opening his bedroom door, he listened to see if anyone was awake, but there was no noise. He tiptoed barefoot down the hallway toward the front door. He nibbled on his bottom lip, wincing when the lock clicking open sounded loud in the deafening silence around him. He quietly pushed open the screen door just enough to slip through, catching it before it could bang against the jamb.

Settling easily into the porch swing, he set it to gently rocking with his toe and lit up the cigarette, inhaling deeply. He almost sighed with pleasure as he felt the smoke invading his lungs, that first pleasant sting after being without one for so long. He could hear some crickets that were still awake in the early morning hours, and the subtle shifting of horse hooves on the ground from Mantacor. The horse intrigued him. Every day since Logan had told him about the horse, he'd gone out after cleaning up the breakfast dishes and stood with the horse, watching him move around the enclosure. He always brought something—a carrot, apple, or sugar cube—with him for the horse, and the animal had begun to realize that. Every day the horse trusted him a little bit more, and just that morning Mantacor had raced over to the fence when he saw Kaden approaching.

Once the horse ate the treat, he would back away from him, but Kaden would stand there and watch the animal. Eventually the horse would make his way to him like that first day, letting Kaden stroke his muzzle or neck. He felt a little guilty for not saying anything, but if he told Logan, he might get mad at him for disobeying his words that night. He didn't want to make the older man mad or cause him to worry. It wasn't like he actually went into the paddock with the horse. He just liked to watch him. It comforted him, like watching a poem or beautiful song in motion—the strong graceful neck, the long strides, the tail rising high in the air as the horse pranced with its mane flaring out behind him when he chose to run. The sheer beauty of the horse more than defied the ugliness of his scar.

A noise to his left brought his head around, and he saw Logan standing in the doorway, the screen door casting deeper shadows over him. "Couldn't sleep?" the man asked huskily.

Kaden shook his head and sheepishly showed him the cigarette. Logan pushed open the screen door and stepped out onto the porch, moving over to settle his long length beside Kaden. "Those are bad for you, you know."

"I know. I don't smoke very often. Only...." He trailed off and looked away.

"I used to smoke, but I quit about three years ago. A close friend of our family wound up with lung cancer from smoking for twenty years. We watched him slowly wither and die. It was a terrible thing to see and made me realize that I wanted to be around to see my family and friends. I didn't want to do that to them," Logan said meaningfully, looking out into the inky blackness surrounding the house.

Kaden smiled ruefully and leaned over to stub out the cigarette on the underside of the railing, setting it aside to take it to the trash. Logan gave him a pleased smile, and pleasure invaded Kaden. He didn't understand why, but he wanted to make the cowboy happy. They sat there in companionable silence for a while, just occasionally setting the swing to rocking. Logan broke the silence to explain about Sunday being his day off. "Sundays are your days off. You won't need to cook, and you can do whatever you want. Read, swim, or Shea mentioned she wanted to teach you to ride, so maybe you could do that."

"Swim?" Kaden asked, surprised because he hadn't seen a pool on the property.

"Yeah, I know you haven't exactly explored much, but we have a pond nearby where you can swim. Maybe all three of us can go, and we'll make a day of it, picnic lunch and all," Logan said excitedly.

Kaden shook his head furiously. "I...can't swim," he confessed, embarrassed to admit that to the larger man.

"Well, then, we can teach you," Logan said proudly, smiling encouragingly at Kaden.

"I... guess that would be okay," he said, caving, letting the man have his way.

The big man grinned broadly and gave a pleased nod. They lapsed into silence again, but then Logan astounded Kaden. "And who told you to go in my room?" he asked suddenly.

"But... uh... I thought I am supposed to clean too!" Kaden exclaimed. "I'm sorry. I didn't mean to do anything wrong. I—" But his tirade of words cut off when he saw the teasing glint in

Logan's eyes. "Don't be mean," he admonished softly. "I thought I did something wrong."

"Aww. I'm sorry. I just couldn't resist. Thank you. I know I'm a bit of a slob. But it's mostly because of lack of time to do everything." Logan sighed. "I appreciate it. A lot. You don't really have to clean. I'm sure Terry told you that because he knows how busy we get at this time, and I never have the chance to do the house cleaning and all. Usually one of the ladies from town will come in a couple times a week. But she's been ill so it's been piling up."

"I don't mind. If I just had to cook I'd go out of my mind with nothing to do. I enjoyed it. And I have to say, your room had to be the worst of them all." Kaden wrinkled his nose at Logan, unaware of how cute it made him look or the thoughts suddenly running through Logan's mind about wanting to kiss him.

Logan cleared his throat and grinned sheepishly. "I told you. I'm a bit of a slob. Mom always had to threaten me to get me to clean my room when I was a kid too. I prefer to be outdoors instead of inside on beautiful days or even rainy days."

They continued to talk for a little while longer. Kaden loved being able to see a side of Logan that he hadn't seen yet, the playful side. The more he learned about the bigger man, the more attracted he became. It occurred to him that when he left Montana it would be more than probable that he would be leaving his heart behind. In the past week, he'd seen Logan treat everyone around him with kindness and respect, treat the animals and horses with gentle hands, and even treat Kaden with that same tenderness. Ignoring his thoughts of leaving, he stood up and stretched, yawning. "I need to get breakfast going, otherwise I might upset the herd."

Logan watched the boy for a moment, studying the slim form and graceful way he moved. The impulse to lean over and kiss him had been strong, but also shocking. He didn't know how to handle these thoughts and emotions he had around this young man before him. It was new territory to him. That, and the boy wasn't exactly open to being touched. He still had more than two and a half months to figure it out and to gain Kaden's trust. Hopefully in that short amount of time he could gain the boy's affections too.

"I think I'll go take a shower and get dressed. Long day today." With that said, he stood and allowed Kaden to enter the house first. His eyes were drawn to his slender backside, a backside that his hands would love to fully explore.

Saturday passed peacefully. Kaden finished up Logan's laundry, folding and putting everything away, including his boxers and underwear. It still felt weird handling the older man's drawers, but he supposed that it was all part of the job. He felt exhausted by the time he'd finished the dishes from the dinner meal. He could barely keep his eyes open as he washed. As soon as the last dish had been put away, he trudged into his room, fell crosswise across the bed, and passed out into a dreamless, deep sleep.

The sound of someone knocking on his bedroom door woke him from the first restful sleep he'd had in a long time. Stumbling from the bed, he opened the door to stare blankly up at Logan. Logan smiled softly and slowly reached out to brush a lock of his hair back into place. "Time to get up." Kaden nodded dumbly and turned to go into the adjoining bathroom, shutting the door behind him.

Logan chuckled quietly at the image the teen made. The sleep-softened expression, his hair disheveled as though... his breath hitched at the idea that had just run through his mind, and he shook his head to clear it. He turned around and headed to the kitchen to make up the lunch for the three of them. Shea bounded down the stairs a few moments later. "Where's Kaden?"

"Still getting ready. I think he actually slept the whole night last night," he told her quietly.

"That's great! I hear him at night, moving around in his room sometimes," she confessed, her expression troubled.

Logan nodded and continued with constructing several sandwiches, wrapping them up, and placing them in the old-fashioned picnic basket his mother had always loved. Then he added some of the leftover potato salad from the other day, paper plates, napkins, forks, and some of the cookies that Kaden had baked yesterday. Placing that by the front door, he grabbed the small cooler and put in some cans of soda and bottles of iced tea before covering them with ice. He added that to the stuff by the door, which already included a blanket for them to sit on and towels to dry off with. He was loading the truck when Kaden came walking down the hallway, yawning tiredly. He blinked owlishly at the sight of everything already completed. "You should have let me do that," he complained.

"Everyone deserves a day off. Don't sweat it," Logan replied, slinging the blanket and towels over his arm. "Are you ready? Wait, don't you have shorts?"

"Huh?" Kaden looked down at his jeans, one knee torn and the other frayed. "Oh… no. I don't like to wear shorts."

"Here, hold these and wait a minute." The cowboy handed him the stuff in his arms and took the stairs two at a time back to the second floor. Thirty seconds later, Logan came dashing back downstairs. He thrust a pair of shorts at Kaden. "These should fit. They're from when I was in high school."

Kaden stared at the blue and white shorts that Logan held out to him. The thought of wearing something that had been close to the man's skin sent a shudder of awareness through him, and he reluctantly took the clothing from him. He swiftly turned around, racing back down to his room, and slammed the door behind him. He leaned his back against the hard wood and stared down at the shorts again. A shiver raced down his spine. Trying to ignore it, he stripped off his sneakers and jeans and stepped into the shorts before putting his jeans back on over them. In the middle of retying his shoes, he froze. Swimming meant that he would have to take off his shirt. And then they would see. No, he couldn't let them. Not that. He'd just leave his shirt on and swim with it. That decided, he grabbed an extra T-shirt from the closet before going back out into the living room.

"All right, then! Let's go," Logan said happily, glad to be able to spend some time with Kaden. Maybe this would be his chance to get to know the kid a little more. "Since you can't ride yet, we'll take the truck."

Kaden was thankful that Shea sat in between him and Logan. Trying to keep his relief from being obvious, he kept his expression carefully blank and stared out the windshield as the vehicle started rolling. It didn't take more than five minutes to get to the pond by truck, and he gazed around curiously as he slid down from the seat, taking in the large body of water, a couple of trees around it, and the mountains in the back. He was awed by the breathtaking beauty and couldn't help but stop and stare. "I look at it that exact same way every time I come out here," Logan said bemusedly, coming to stand by his side to stare out over the land with a prideful expression.

"I've never seen anywhere more beautiful," Kaden replied with wonder, his fingers itching to write as he looked at the white mist that clung to the tip of the mountains. He wished he had brought his notebook along. Tilting his head back slightly and to the right, he looked up at Logan, who stood gazing out over the land with a content look on his face. "You really love it here, don't you?" he queried.

"Yes. Very much." The cowboy tipped his head slightly to look down at Kaden. "Ready to start your swimming lessons?"

Reluctantly, Kaden nodded and followed the bigger man toward the water, stopping to toe off his sneakers and take off his pants. As he stood there in shorts, bare feet, and the T-shirt, he turned and practically stopped breathing. Logan had stripped down to nothing but his shorts, and his very tan, muscular chest gleamed in the sunlight, rippling with his movements. Kaden swallowed hard as his mouth went dry from the sudden lust invading his body. He didn't notice Shea's speculative gaze on him as he watched Logan. Shaking his head, he looked down at the ground and started with surprise when Logan's deep, honeyed voice washed over him. "Aren't you going to take off your shirt?"

"N... no. I, uh... burn easily," Kaden lied baldly, not wanting them to see the shamefulness of his body.

"Oh... okay. Well, why don't you come into the water until it's about waist high, all right?" Logan moved toward the water, stepping into the dark liquid. He kept walking, sighing with pleasure as the cool water hit his heated skin. Soon he was in the water chest high and turned to see Kaden still standing hesitantly on the bank. "Come on," he called.

Shea swam in the water, keeping her eye on Kaden as she went in circles around her brother. She sensed a certain tension, almost chemistry-like, between her brother and Kaden. Was it possible that Kaden had a crush on her brother? The boy was afraid of men, so it wouldn't make sense. Would it? She watched him stepping slowly into the pond, his eyes locked on the surface as he continued to move forward until the water had reached his waist, and he refused to go any further. She swam toward him and stopped beside him. "Keep going. I'm right here. Hold onto my arm." She urged him deeper into the water.

Logan stayed where he was, watching Kaden and Shea moving closer to where he stood. Once they were by Logan's side, Shea let go of Kaden because he was still able to stand, and started to demonstrate how to move his arms and kick his legs.

Eventually, Kaden was able to keep himself afloat and began to enjoy himself. The siblings watched with amusement and heady warmth flooded them as they watched his expression of pure joy and pride. Kaden acted like a little kid on Christmas morning, and yet it was something so simple to accomplish. It brought a humble feeling upon their shoulders about how good their lives had been and how much they truly had been blessed.

Kaden waded back to the shallows and watched Logan and Shea splashing and dunking one another. He watched the love and affection they had for one another and felt envious of it. Shame followed quickly on its heels. Being envious because they were happy wasn't fair to them. They deserved to be happy. With a sigh, he turned and walked out of the water to collapse on the blanket Logan had spread out. He lay on his back staring up at the wisps of clouds strolling across the sky and became lost in his thoughts. Slowly his eyelids began to droop and his breathing evened out. Within moments he fell asleep, unconsciously turning on his side.

Shea and Logan gave up the fight over who could dunk who more times and decided to get out and eat lunch. They smiled at each other when they saw that Kaden had fallen asleep. Both of them collapsed onto the blanket next to Kaden. Logan's eyes traced the length of the boy's body, studying the thin but muscular legs and the slender back. That's when he noticed Kaden's feet. The soles of his feet were covered in round scars that looked like burn marks. His eyes widened, and his breath caught at the realization of what could have caused them. His own father used to smoke cigars. Logan's jaw clenched, and his lips tightened in anger. If he ever got his hands on the son of a bitch who'd hurt such a gentle person, he'd rip them into shreds and bury them somewhere out in the mountains where no one could ever find them. Kaden shifted in his sleep and rolled to his back, one hand resting on his stomach and the other flinging out to land close to Logan.

The cowboy's eyes narrowed in on the leather wristband and saw how it dug into his wrist. An irritated red patch was showing around the edges. In an effort to make the boy more comfortable, he carefully and slowly unsnapped and pulled it off, staring in horror at the marks that lay beneath. Shea let out a soft gasp of shock and lifted a hand to her mouth. "Logan," she whispered in alarm.

He gave her a look to silence her and carefully replaced the wristband, wondering what the hell was going on with Kaden. There were old scars and marks that looked fresh, as though done only recently. His hands balled into fists, anger coursing through his veins. Did someone make those marks on him? Did he do it himself? How did they get there? Dammit. He felt so helpless, like he couldn't do anything for the younger man. When they returned to the house, he would have to talk to Kaden. Someone had to stop him before he seriously hurt himself.

Pulling the picnic basket closer, Logan began to take everything out before gently shaking Kaden by the shoulder. "Kaden. Time to eat. Wake up."

A voice called to him in the darkness, and Kaden opened his eyes slowly to find Logan partially leaning over him. Fear flashed through him for a second, but then it dissipated. He stared up at Logan, blinking several times to clear the sleep from his eyes. "It's time to eat, Kaden," Logan repeated, taking his hand away and leaning back again.

Kaden's brow furrowed. Something was wrong. An odd look glittered in Logan's eyes and a tenseness in his body, as if he were angry about something. Sitting up, he glanced over at Shea and saw that she looked pale and upset. "Is something wrong?" he asked in concern.

"No. Everything's fine. Do you want soda or iced tea?" Logan responded in a flat tone.

Logan's face was tense, and Kaden knew he wasn't telling him the truth. Had he spoken in his sleep and said something? Were they mad that he didn't join in on the dunking games or because he'd fallen asleep? With a sigh, he took the sandwich from Logan and pointed at a soda, moving back to lean against the tree behind him. He stared off into the distance at the mountains as he nibbled at the sandwich, his appetite gone and his stomach twisting painfully. Maybe Logan had grown tired of his problems. Was he going to kick him out and send him home? He finally gave up the pretense of eating and dropped the sandwich back into its wrapping before closing it up and placing it beside him. "Did I do something wrong?"

"No. Why do you think that?" The cowboy's voice was stiff and emotionless.

"Because you're angry, and Shea's upset. Obviously something's not right, and you don't want to talk about it at the moment. That's fine. But tell me now, are you going to fire me and send me back to New York?" Kaden asked bluntly, tiredly, his eyes dull as they locked with Logan's.

"No!" Both of them exclaimed at once. "We're just concerned about you," Logan continued cautiously. "Where did those marks on your wrist come from?"

Kaden stiffened, and his eyes opened wide as he realized that Logan had seen the cuts on his wrist. He brought his arm with the wristband close to his chest and looked away from the siblings. They had discovered the one thing he was most ashamed of. "How did you know?" he murmured.

"I took off the armband when I saw that it was irritating your arm. I put it back on because I didn't intend to talk to you about it out here. But I don't want you to think that I'm going to send you away. I'm just worried and so is Shea," Logan explained gently, his gaze sad and concerned. "Why do you have those marks on

69

your arm?"

Picking at the hem of his T-shirt, Kaden didn't respond right away, but when he did both Shea and Logan felt as though the wind had been knocked out of them. "It's the only way that the pain goes away. When I have a panic attack, it's a reflex reaction to that pain. I… cut or scratch myself."

"Oh, Kaden," Shea breathed, moving to his side to hug him tightly. She stroked his hair back from his face tenderly and held him tighter. "You have to stop. You could seriously hurt yourself one day. Please, for me, promise you'll try to stop. If you feel the urge, come talk to me or Logan. We'll help you through it, Kaden. But please don't hurt yourself anymore." She was practically begging by the end of her statement, and Kaden buried his face in her shoulder, embarrassed at his actions.

A strong hand came to rest gently on his other shoulder, and then Logan's voice came from close by. "It's nothing to be ashamed of, Kaden. We all look for outlets in our lives when something upsets us or makes us feel pain. But that's not a healthy outlet. If you need something, I can show you a few judo moves that can help release your frustration or pain. We can set up an area where you can beat the hell out of a stuffed dummy or something, anything else but this." His hands traveled down Kaden's arm to his wrist, touching the skin just above the armband lightly.

Kaden shivered at the heat that traversed his arm along with the skin of that rough hand. "I'm sorry," he choked, squeezing his eyes shut tightly.

"There's nothing to be sorry for," Shea said fiercely, pulling back to look him in the face. "I know that you aren't ready to talk to us about anything that has happened to you, and I understand that, but I think if you do it might help the pain fade away. Even though you've only been here a few days, I already feel like we've known you our entire lives, and we really care about you. Even if

70

you never talk to us about it, please stop hurting yourself. Promise me," she demanded.

The trembling boy studied his legs for a moment, wondering if he would have the strength to keep the promise. But he slowly nodded, still not meeting their eyes for fear of seeing rejection or pity. He couldn't take it if they felt pity for him. "I'll try." He saw the look that Shea gave him. "It's the best I can do. It's… a knee-jerk reaction, Shea. I can't always control it."

Logan had mostly been silent while Shea talked, but this time he spoke up. "Please try. For us."

Kaden nodded again and smiled tremulously at Logan. "I will."

The siblings seemed to almost wilt with relief, and they started to joke around, including Kaden in it as well, as they finished their lunch. Finally, they headed back to the ranch. Shea instructed him to change his clothes and be back at the barn in twenty minutes or she'd come after him. Kaden laughed at her words, knowing that she didn't have the strength to force him. As the foreign sound issued from Kaden's throat, he was turning and moving toward the house, unaware of the green eyes studying him or the way the sound of his laughter affected the owner of those eyes.

Chapter 7

WHEN Kaden had finished changing, he went back outside to meet Shea. As he approached, he saw her leading a saddled horse out of the barn. A slightly smaller horse than Mantacor, she had a beautiful copper-red coat, almost like flames. A dark brown mane and tail shifted as she walked. Shea smiled at Kaden and motioned him forward to where she and the horse stood. He approached cautiously, keeping his eyes on the horse. "This is Brandy. She's two years old and very gentle and easy to learn with. Come closer and hold out your hand for her to smell you. It's how they get to know you."

Kaden reluctantly lifted his hand, extending it out to the horse palm up. The horse settled her nose against his palm, and he could feel the whiskers around her nose tickling his palm. His lips curved into a smile, and his eyes started to twinkle with laughter and delight. "She's very beautiful."

"Now, you should only mount a horse from the left side. Take the reins in your left hand." Shea handed him the reins, and he placed them in his left hand, nervously shifting his feet as she positioned him beside the horse. "Good. Now place your left hand, holding the reins, on the saddle, or you can also hold the mane. There are no nerve endings connected to the mane, so you don't have to worry about hurting her."

He did as she indicated and waited for further instructions. "Okay, now place your right hand on the rear of the saddle. Just like that. Good. Place your left foot in the stirrup. Now bounce three times, and then pull yourself up, swinging your leg over the saddle as you do so."

Kaden almost dropped the reins and had to attempt this several times as he tried to follow her instructions. Finally in the saddle, he panted from the exertion of attempting to mount the horse. He gripped the saddle and reins tightly, realizing how far off the ground he actually sat. It looked like a long way down. The horse shifted, and he let out a squeak, suddenly gripping the horse's mane tightly. Shea laughed, her eyes crinkling at the corners and a dimple appearing in the corner of her mouth. "Relax, Kaden. The horse can sense if you're nervous, and it will make her nervous."

Forcing himself to relax, he slowly eased his grip on the mane and watched as Shea went around to the other side of the horse to make sure his foot was in the stirrup. He'd instinctively slid his foot in upon mounting. She adjusted the length to his leg, making sure it rested lightly against the horse's side. "Now I'm going to lead you into the corral over there and we're just going to do a steady walk. Okay, Kaden?"

When Shea started walking the horse, Kaden's legs tightened, and he tensed. The movements of the horse frightened him, and the thought of falling off came to the front of his mind. "Loosen your legs before you cut off her air supply," he heard that deep voice call from nearby. Kaden brought his head up to find Logan sitting on the fence, his hands on the board beside him and his legs resting on the next one down.

Logan's eyes were hooded with some kind of emotion that Kaden couldn't identify, and he looked away uneasily. He tried to instead concentrate on the animal beneath him and Shea's instructions. She walked with them around the corral several times, letting them get used to the rhythm of each other. When she felt that they had a good rapport, she stopped near Logan.

"Okay, now I'm going to give you the opportunity to walk her on your own. Just squeeze her sides lightly with your legs and gently rock your hips forward. That will get her going in a walk. Don't try anything else right away. You have to get used to the effect of riding a horse and the motions."

Kaden nodded, doing as she indicated, and when the horse started walking, he looked nervously at Shea, but she only smiled encouragingly. As the horse walked around the corral with just him, he kept glancing at Shea and Logan, finding them talking about something serious. He wondered if it pertained to him, and he frowned, looking down at where his hands held the reins. It didn't mean they were talking about him. He decided to just ignore it and enjoy his time here as much as he could. With a resolved frame of mind, he looked up, smiling as the horse neared Logan and Shea.

"When you want the horse to stop, pull back gently on the reins. But don't forget those are attached to the horse's mouth and could hurt the horse if you pull too hard," Shea explained as he drew close to them.

Doing as instructed, he pulled lightly on the reins, and the horse stopped, shifting from foot to foot beneath him. "Now how do I get down?" he asked.

"Just swing your right leg over the back of the horse and drop down with that leg before removing your left foot from the stirrup," Logan said, intercepting Shea's response. He watched the way the slight muscles on Kaden's frame rippled as he dismounted easily with the strength in his legs. "You did good, kid."

Kaden almost preened under his compliments, grinning broadly. In less than a week, the haunted look in his eyes had begun to fade, and Logan felt an immense sense of relief and happiness that he could help the teenager heal. He didn't analyze or examine the other feelings that were building inside him. The boy was only here for three months, then he'd go back to New York, and Logan wouldn't have to worry about these feelings Kaden was stirring up. But the thought of Kaden going back to New York made his heart twinge and his stomach clench. Suddenly angry with himself, Logan jumped down off the fence with a gruff, "I've got some bookkeeping to take care of. I'll see you guys at dinner." He turned on his heel and left.

"Did I do something wrong?" Kaden muttered, looking down at the ground.

"No. You didn't do anything wrong. He's just tired, is all. He gets like that when he's tired," Shea lied, looking after her brother with a harsh glare. Why did he insist on ignoring his own emotions? And now he'd upset Kaden. "Come on. Let me show you how to groom her and unsaddle her. The next lesson, I'll show you how to saddle her, okay? That way you can do it for yourself."

They unsaddled and brushed Brandy down, making sure she was clean and happy before leading her into the stall. The sun hung low in the sky, right above the edge of the mountains, when they headed back to the house. For the first time since he'd been a child, Kaden felt safe. Love and tenderness didn't exist in Kaden's barren life. He'd lost hope in ever having them again because of the many harsh realities he'd been forced to confront at an early age. His faith in a lot of things had died the same day they'd laid his mother in the ground, including his belief in God. What kind of cruel God would allow his life to continue the way it did? The need to be alone for a while came over him, and he made an excuse to Shea before going into his bedroom and shutting the door.

Grabbing his notebook, he lay down on his stomach on the bed and began to write—about the mountains and the big open sky from that morning, about the horseback-riding lesson, and the big man who seemed to never be far from his mind but would never understand. The lyrics just flowed from his fingers, and by the time he looked up, the clock read seven thirty, and the sky had darkened. He placed his pen in the book and closed the cover, standing and stretching with a soft moan. His back ached from the long time spent in one position. He decided to go make something for dinner for everyone and went into the kitchen to find Shea already cooking. Stopping in surprise, he watched her for a moment. She was making simple boxed macaroni and cheese, so she should be all right with that. He figured, anyway.

The water started boiling, and because she was too busy digging through the fridge, it foamed up and began to spill over. Kaden rushed over to the stove and turned the temperature down, ensuring that the water level dropped before moving away again. "I'm sorry. I should have been out here to do this," he told Shea, moving to take over, but she refused to let him do it and forced him to go sit down.

"I'm fine. I just didn't notice that the water was already boiling. Like Logan said, everyone needs a day off." She dumped in the elbow macaroni and stirred it to make sure it didn't stick to the bottom of the pan.

Kaden wondered if Logan was still in his study and rested his chin in his hand as he watched Shea darting around the kitchen. He'd seemed so agitated earlier. What had happened to upset him? It seemed like he had gotten angry. The thought pained him, and he nibbled at his bottom lip in concern. Without realizing it, he let out a sigh and then jumped in alarm when he heard that honeyed voice he'd already begun to crave. "Why the big sigh?"

Turning his head, he saw Logan leaning against the doorjamb, his arms crossed against his chest and a tired look to his face. "Nothing. Just thinking is all."

Logan nodded briefly and moved toward Shea to help her by setting out plates and glasses for drinks. He kept glancing at

Kaden, watching him carefully to see if he would reveal any of his inner thoughts on his face. The boy was good at hiding his emotions for the most part, except for when it came to fear. Fear seemed to be ingrained in the teenager, and he was glad that he hadn't seen that emotion from Kaden at all that day.

The three of them sat down to eat. Most of the meal went by silently with a few words injected here and there. Unable to take the silence anymore, Shea let out a sound of frustration before dumping her plate in the sink and leaving. Logan watched her go with an uncaring expression before turning back to look at Kaden. "So you've been here almost a week now. How do you like it?"

Looking up from his bowl, Kaden smiled softly. "I think this is the best place I've ever been. It's beautiful, quiet, and you and Shea are the kindest people I've ever met. When I leave in a few months, I'm going to miss you guys." With that he stood up, walked over to the sink, and placed his bowl in before starting the water.

Something akin to dismay prodded at Logan, telling him to tell Kaden he didn't have to leave. Before he could make a fool of himself, Logan stood and moved over to Kaden's side to drop his plate in the sink. He noticed that Kaden didn't jump this time, and grinned like an idiot on the way out of the kitchen.

Kaden finished up the dishes before going to bed. He'd started sleeping more now, every night for at least a few hours even if not the whole night. He hadn't been lying to Logan when he said he would miss him, his sister, and the ranch. It was a beautiful place to live, and he could only dream of staying here. His mind knew that it wasn't right, what his heart longed for. To keep from having his heart broken yet again he would have to distance himself, but it might already be too late. He put away the few dishes and snapped off the light, walking to his bedroom. Something told him this would be another restless night.

A couple of weeks went by with the same routine. Kaden, of course, making the meals during the six days the men were out on the ranch, and also Shea kept giving him his riding lessons. He still went out to see Mantacor in the mornings after the men left. The horse had really started to trust him, and he was trying to keep it from being obvious whenever Shea or Logan happened to be around. The horse would stand at the fence and call for him, nickering quietly and pacing back and forth, watching him. It made him feel guilty that he couldn't say hello or go over and rub his nose. But he knew Logan would be really upset with him.

To his distress, Logan found out. It was about a month into his reign as cook on the ranch, and he went out right after the men left, practically racing to the fence where the horse stood waiting for him. "Hey there, Mantacor," he crooned softly, laughing quietly as the horse lapped up the sugar cubes in his palm. He patted the side of his neck and laughed louder as the horse nuzzled at his neck.

"What the hell do you think you're doing?" He heard that deep voice shouting from across the distance, and Kaden saw Logan racing toward him, causing him to back away from the advancing figure in fear.

"Didn't I tell you to stay away from him? He's dangerous!" He was shouting at Kaden and without thinking, reached out to grab Kaden's arm lightly.

Kaden froze. He wondered if Logan intended to hit him and closed his eyes tightly, seeming to scrunch in on himself. Logan realized with horror what Kaden thought and immediately let him go, clenching his hands into fists at his side. "I would think after being around me for the last four weeks you would have figured out by now that I would never, ever hit you, Kaden." His voice was dangerously low, and Kaden sensed that he'd hurt the older man.

"Stay away from that horse." With that, the cowboy spun

around and stomped to the tool shed behind the barn.

Anger radiated from Logan as Kaden watched the stiff, broad back moving away from him. He didn't understand how he had the power to hurt Logan like that. It wasn't like he was anything other than an employee to him. But he knew guilt made him think that, and he tried to repress his mental voice telling him to run, fast and far. Maybe it would just be better if he disappeared from their lives. He had brought nothing but problems and trouble to the siblings, even though they had been kind and gentle from the start. His hand rose instinctively to his cheek, his fingers drifting over the ragged edges of the scar there. It had been awhile since he'd remembered that it existed, and touching it made him remember why he shouldn't get too close to anyone.

Resolve stiffening his spine, Kaden went into the house, packed the duffel bag he'd brought with him and headed back into the kitchen to make the lunch for the men. He set it out on the table with covers over it to make sure no flies landed on it. Then he threw together dinner and placed it in the oven before quickly writing instructions on paper for Logan to finish up. Knowing that he owed the man a lot, he sat down to write an appropriate thank-you. He wrote of how much he'd loved the time he'd spent on the ranch, and how sorry he was for all the trouble he had caused. He went on to explain that the horse had come to trust him, letting him touch him willingly, and even anticipated his visits each day. He apologized for disobeying Logan's orders, but he had been drawn to the horse because they were a lot alike. Trust did not come easily.

He propped the letter against the oven timer in the middle of the stove, grabbed his duffel bag from his room, and walked out the front door, but not without looking back for a split second. With a heavy heart, he began his long walk to town. Logan had given him his pay each week, and it rested in the bottom of his duffel bag. He had enough to get back to New York and find an apartment. Maybe it would be a good idea just to go somewhere else. Terry would probably be mad at him for abandoning another job. The sun beat down on him, sweat popping out over his forehead, upper lip, and beneath his arms, but Kaden trudged on, shrugging the bag higher up onto his shoulders. Damn, it was hot. Hopefully, he would be back to town and gone by the time Logan came back for lunch. Only Kaden didn't count on the fact that Logan would come back to apologize to him.

Kaden reached the town about a half-hour after he left the house because someone stopped to pick him up, giving him a lift. When he hopped down out of the truck, he thanked the guy behind the wheel and turned around to find the dark-haired lady from that night at the bar coming out of a beauty salon. "You're Kaden, aren't you?" she asked when she spotted him, heading his way with a smile.

He nodded mutely, wondering what she wanted. "I'm Helen Chambers. I saw you that night at the honky-tonk. We didn't have a chance to meet because of that bastard Franklin." She held out her hand, and he shook it cautiously, studying her. "What are you doin' in town? Charlie bring you in to get more supplies?" She looked around to see if she could spot the ranch truck.

"No. I'm going home," Kaden said softly.

"Oh? How come? The roundup isn't over for another couple of months, and I know for a fact that Logan would never fire you. He loves your cooking too much. He told me how happy he is that his cousin Terry suggested he give you the job. It's been hard getting someone in to do such a heavy load." Helen laughed lightly. She saw the haunted look that Logan spoke of the last time they had talked. And she had a feeling this young man was the reason that he hadn't been around lately. Something in the way he spoke about him, and the look he got in his eyes, gave her that impression. She would never figure a big, masculine man such as Logan would be interested in another man, but it appeared that

80

way. Granted, the kid did look a little on the feminine side.

"I just need to go home is all," he lied, not wanting to tell her the truth.

"Well, that would be a real shame, baby, because those Michaels siblings really like you, and I think they'd miss you like crazy if you left. Of course, it is your choice, but at least think about sayin' goodbye before you do." Her voice held a serious note, and she reached out to lightly touch his unblemished cheek. "If you need someone to give you a lift to the airport, Walter Moseby's headin' that way to pick up his daughter. I'm sure he'd be willin' to give ya a lift."

Kaden looked down at the ground, his mind turning over her words and the implication behind them. Was it true? Would they miss him? No one had ever missed him before, and it caused an uncomfortable feeling to settle over his heart. If you listened really hard, you probably could have heard the ice cracking as it slowly melted a tiny bit more. Tears threatened, and he blinked hard, forcing them away. Lifting his head, he smiled shyly at her and nodded. "I think I'll go back, like you said. Thank you, Miss Chambers."

"It's Helen, and don't mention it, kid. You want a lift back?" she drawled, smiling at him and motioning to where her truck sat nearby.

He nodded enthusiastically and followed her to the truck. He spotted Logan's truck as he reached to open the passenger door. Closing his eyes for a split second, he hung his head, knowing Logan would most likely start yelling at him. He opened his eyes to smile weakly at Helen and indicated Logan with a toss of his chin, stepping back from the truck. "I guess he found out already. Thank you for the offer, Mi…uh… Helen."

"You take care, Kaden. I'm sure he'll settle down. He's a good man with a very big heart in that broad chest of his. Don't worry too much if he acts like a bear with a thorn in its paw. He likes you a lot." She winked at him before laughing at the I-swallowed-a-fish expression that came over the man's face because he'd sensed the meaning behind her words. She climbed up in the truck and pulled away from the curb, waving at Logan as she drove by.

Logan pulled up to the curb beside Kaden, leaned over, and shoved the door open roughly. "Get in," he demanded in a low voice.

Kaden winced and stepped up into the truck, saying immediately, "Before you yell at me, I couldn't go. Helen offered me a ride back to the ranch. I'm sorry."

The cowboy stayed quiet for a few moments, his hands clenched on the wheel and his knuckles white from the tension. Finally, he broke the silence. "Why?" That was all he said, one word.

It flooded Kaden with guilt, and he looked down at his hands resting in his lap. "Because I don't want to cause you and Shea trouble. I've already caused more than one problem in your life, and you guys don't deserve that after all the wonderful and kind things you've done for me. I didn't want to pay you back by doing something to make it harder on you."

"And you think that by leaving like that, without a word or without even saying goodbye, that it wouldn't be making it harder on me? Dammit, Kaden. I—" He stopped himself, tightening his jaw and biting his tongue.

"I'm sorry, Logan. I really am. Give me another chance, please? I promise to try harder," Kaden pleaded, wondering if maybe this would be his final chance to be with the cowboy.

"I'm not going to send you away, Kaden, if that's what you're thinking." Logan sighed. "I already told you that before, and I've already told you that I want to help you. I... didn't tell you this before because I didn't want to scare you or make you want to leave sooner, but I want you to stay on after the roundup. We'll continue with the same arrangement, except you'll just be cooking for me, Shea, Charlie, and two other hands that stay on year-round."

Kaden stared at him in amazement, floored that Logan would be offering him something so wonderful: an opportunity to become part of a team, a chance to become friends, and a place to heal. It left him speechless, and he saw the furtive glances Logan sent his way, as well as the worried look that crossed the older man's face. "I... I don't know what to say. I can't believe that you actually want me to stay around even after all the trouble I've already caused you."

"You aren't trouble, Kaden. I'm sorry I yelled at you like that. I should have controlled my temper a little better. But things happen, and that's everyday life. For about three weeks now, nothing happened, right? And besides, you stated in your letter that Mantacor seems to like you. Well, if that's true, then maybe you can help me with him, and that way you can earn your keep, hmm?" Logan teased, noting the tension easing from Kaden's body and the happy glow that started to invade his eyes. Relief swamped him. If he hadn't come back to apologize, Kaden might have already left. The idea of Kaden not being around with his sweet smile and lilting voice didn't sit well.

"Really? That would be great! He's such a sweet horse! He truly is! And I know that if he got to know you, he'd like you too!" Kaden practically bounced in his seat and looked over at Logan, grinning widely.

Logan nodded, just listening to Kaden chattering about the horse and how every morning he went out with a treat to greet the horse, spending time with him. It made him feel good to hear that voice, because it sounded so cheerful and carefree. His heart had gone out to the boy when he'd first arrived, seeing the scar on his cheek and the ones on his feet. He knew that the kid hadn't tried to hurt himself again because the wristband had been removed after the cuts healed and hadn't been replaced. Throughout the past month, he'd been getting to know Kaden a little better and learning a teeny bit of his life in New York, at least whatever the kid would tell him. He'd slowly lost the objections that had gone through his mind when he'd admitted his attraction. He'd come to accept the fact that he wanted Kaden, and that he desired him more than any woman he'd ever been attracted to. It scared him a little, the intensity of his feelings for the younger man, and the lust he felt whenever he saw him, but he'd accepted it. He found it getting harder and harder not to act on his attraction. Especially when the man looked like he did at that very moment. Happy.

He wanted to touch him, hold him, and kiss him. Fear of scaring or upsetting Kaden kept him away. But it frustrated him, and he was taking it out on the men. They'd been complaining to Charlie about his attitude lately, and the way he rode them hard about their work, especially how he snapped at them for the littlest things. It wore on his nerves, and they were beginning to fray, ready to snap at any moment.

CHAPTER 8

THE truck pulled into the ranch, and Shea stood on the porch, anxiously awaiting their return. As soon as she saw Kaden in the truck, she felt the tension leave her body, and she raced down the steps, launching herself at Kaden as soon as he stepped down from the truck. He staggered at the weight against him, and he hugged her, breathing the scent of shampoo in deeply. "I'm sorry, Shea," he whispered into her hair, holding her tightly.

When she pulled back to look at him, there were tears in her eyes, and he immediately felt worse. "Please don't cry, Shea. I couldn't bear that. I'm sorry. I wasn't really going to leave. As soon as I got to town, I knew I made a mistake. I had to come back."

"You jerk! Don't ever do that again!" She hugged him again, sniffling to try and keep her tears from falling.

He laughed. "I won't. I promise."

"I need to get back out there. They're probably wondering where I am. I'll see you guys at dinner," Logan said, leaning out of the window, and then he drove off to wherever the men went every day.

Kaden stared after him, still wondering if everything would

be okay between them. He gave Shea a smile and walked up the steps beside her. The first thing he did was put his things away again. Shea didn't seem to want to let him out of her sight, so she trailed him to his room, sitting on his bed and watching him while he unpacked. She questioned him on the notebooks, but he just shrugged it off and put them in the top drawer of the dresser. Once he'd completed putting his meager belongings away, she'd followed him to the kitchen and helped him set up the preparations for dinner. She insisted on eating lunch with him. He washed up the few dishes they'd used, and then motioned for Shea to follow him from the house.

He took her to the corral that Mantacor was in. "The reason I left this morning is because Logan found out the secret I've been hiding. I... have been coming to see Mantacor every day, and he's started to trust me."

He indicated for her to stay near the end of the corral, and he walked further away, waiting patiently for the horse to come to him. Although it kept its eye on Shea, it approached Kaden slowly. He held out the sugar cubes in his palm, and the horse lapped them up before bumping its head against his shoulder.

Shea stared in surprise and awe. Her brother had been trying for months and months to get the animal to trust him, but to his frustration and unhappiness, the horse refused to come near him. She couldn't believe that the boy had accomplished in a month what her brother had been trying for almost a year. "I cannot believe it. How?"

"I guess he could sense that we're a lot alike," Kaden explained gently, looking up at the horse and smiling, running his palm down the length of its face. "And I kept coming out here every day, talking to him and giving him treats. Eventually, he started to look forward to my visits, even calling to me or racing to the fence every time he saw me."

"Wow. That's so amazing. Do you think that he would be able to do that with Logan?"

"I… don't know. It will take a lot of time to gain his trust. He's been treated really badly."

"Like you?" Shea questioned softly.

Kaden stiffened, leaning his forehead against the horse's, before slowly and hesitantly giving a small nod. "Yeah. Like me."

He spent the next hour trying to show Mantacor that Shea wouldn't ever hurt him, but he kept shying away from the girl, or would run to the other side of the corral unless she backed away. So Kaden finally gave up after the tenth attempt, and bid the horse goodbye before heading back into the house. Shea stayed as he prepared dinner for everyone. He was just finishing up when the first truck arrived back in the yard. It would still be about fifteen to thirty minutes before everyone came inside, and he hurried to have everything on the table by then. Once again, Shea and Logan sat in the kitchen while the men sat in the dining room.

Exhaustion from the seemingly endless day set in, and Kaden collapsed into his bed gratefully once the dishes had been washed, asleep almost instantly. About two in the morning he jolted awake at a strange sound. Lying there, he waited for it to happen again, and he realized with horror what had caused the sound. A storm raged outside the house, and rain beat against the clapboard side of the building. Lightning lit up his room, and a loud rumble literally shook the windows, causing him to let out a cry of fear and to leap from the bed. Storms terrified him, even now, after all these years. He lunged for the closet, opening the door and slamming it behind him. He scrunched down into the farthest corner, bringing his knees up to his chest, and covered his ears with his hands. Whimpers issued from his throat, because even with his hands over his ears, he could still hear the thunder and feel it in the energy around him.

Logan had also been awakened by the storm, a few minutes before Kaden, and had gotten up to use the bathroom. He'd pulled the sheets back to slip in between the covers when he heard what sounded like a scream. His heart started pounding, and he rushed to Shea's room, quietly opening the door to find her sleeping, curled up beneath the sheets. He took the stairs as quickly but softly as possible, heading toward Kaden's room. The door wasn't locked, and he twisted the handle, easing the door open to peer inside, but the sheets were thrown back and the bed sat empty. He stepped inside and looked around the room. Panic set in, along with the fear that Kaden had decided to leave again. Calming himself, Logan reasoned that Kaden might be somewhere else in the house, so he turned to go look in the kitchen and living room, but a sound stopped him. He realized that it had come from the closet.

Lightning lit up the room again as he opened the closet door and spotted Kaden sitting in the corner of the closet. "Kaden? What's wrong?" He kneeled down in front of Kaden. He could see the shivers wracking the boy's body, and that his eyes were scrunched closed in terror. Reaching out, he gently laid his hand on Kaden's knee. "Kaden? Are you afraid of thunderstorms? Is that it?"

Kaden felt the hand on his knee and looked up to see Logan on his knees in front of him, and without a thought, he launched himself at Logan, his arms wrapping around the man's waist. He felt Logan's arms come around his back, and then he felt himself lifted into Logan's lap like a child as the man adjusted himself to lean against the closet door. "Shh. It's all right. It's only a thunderstorm. It'll be over soon." Logan soothingly ran his hands up and down Kaden's back, almost groaning at how good the younger man felt in his arms and against his body.

Logan could feel the teen shuddering, and when a particularly loud rumble of thunder shook the house on its foundation, the boy let out a mewling cry of fear, pressing tighter against the cowboy. "Kaden, shh. It's nothing to be afraid of. I'm here with you. Calm down."

The storm slowly rolled away, leaving the rain pelting the windows, as Logan continued to hold Kaden and try to comfort him. He tried to concentrate on anything but the firm rear against his crotch. Exquisitely painful, the contact only made him desire Kaden even further. The thin body lying against his was so fragile in his arms, and he almost trembled at the thought of someone hurting such a delicate being. Kaden had buried his face against his throat, and he could feel the warmth of his breath whispering over the skin there, causing his body temperature to rise, and he gritted his teeth, trying to keep from getting aroused. Eventually, the only sounds left in the room were the gentle tapping of misty rain hitting the window panes and the breath issuing from their lungs.

Kaden became aware of being held, and the person who held him. Next he became aware of the deep, earthy scent on the flesh beneath his nose, and he licked at his suddenly dry lips, accidentally brushing over the salty, sensitive skin on Logan's neck. He felt the older man shudder, and Logan's arms tightened briefly. He pulled back to look up at Logan, and tried to smile at him, but it didn't quite make it. Logan's head dipped down close to his, his lips brushing lightly over Kaden's before pulling back. Surprise coursed through Kaden, and he could only stare at the other man, his lips tingling from the slide of skin over skin. Logan reached up a hand to caress Kaden's cheek, ignoring the feeling of the scarred flesh beneath his fingers. Seeing no resistance from Kaden, he leaned forward and pressed his lips more firmly over Kaden's.

He felt the response from Kaden in the soft movement of Kaden's lips under his, and he moaned, flicking his tongue over the plump bottom lip, caressing the skin there. Kaden's eyes opened wide, and he let out a small gasp, heat filling his veins like liquid flames. "Kaden?" Logan questioned hoarsely, his green eyes searching Kaden's violet ones.

Eyes slowly closing, Kaden leaned forward, this time returning the kiss and increasing the intimacy by using his own tongue hesitantly, almost fainting with the sensations that flooded him at the feel of Logan's tongue rubbing along his. It felt so good to be able to kiss Logan. They slowly, languidly made love to each other's mouths, forgetting everything around them as they lost themselves in the kiss. Their hands stayed where they were, just their lips connecting them intimately. They only broke the kiss to gasp for breath. Kaden buried his face back in the crook of Logan's neck, his face flaming in embarrassment.

Logan chuckled softly and ran his fingers through Kaden's hair. "Did you enjoy that?" he asked curiously, and he felt Kaden nod against him. "Good."

He nuzzled at Kaden's ear for a moment, and then reluctantly set Kaden aside and stood, holding his hand out to pull Kaden to his feet. "We should get some more sleep. I'll see you in the morning." He dropped a small kiss on the top of Kaden's head.

Kaden watched in a daze as Logan left the room, his hand unconsciously reaching up to trace the outline of his lips in wonder, but then doubt set in. Had the cowboy only kissed him because he'd been upset? His mind demanded that he believe that, but the half of his heart that had been released from the cage of ice he'd formed around it years ago demanded he acknowledge that the kiss had come after he'd calmed down. So the man must have kissed him because he wanted to. Kaden crawled into bed and lay there until the alarm went off, thinking about what had happened. He'd felt the kiss all the way down to his toes.

Crickets were still chirping when he started preparing breakfast, still slightly bemused from those shared moments with Logan in the darkness. It had been the gentlest, sweetest kiss he'd ever experienced. It left him bewildered that passion could make him feel good, instead of the pain he'd always associated with it. Would Logan regret it once the light of day began to shine? No matter what happened, Kaden would never regret it, or wish it had never happened. He was just setting the plates out for the ranch hands when he heard Logan's boots on the stairs. A flush dusted his high cheekbones when the cowboy stepped into the room, the man's eyes immediately settling on him, and the sensuous lips that had pressed so heatedly against his last night curved up at the corners. Kaden nervously pushed a lock of hair behind his ear before returning the smile, dropping his eyes to the floor.

Logan felt his heart leap in his chest at the shy actions, and he moved toward him, intent on repeating the early morning's events, only to stop in frustration when the sound of boots and men's voices filtered through to him. Kaden darted into the kitchen to get everything set out on the table before they reached the house. Logan gave a strained smile and good morning to his ranch hands. He wanted to speak with Kaden and hoped that Shea would sleep in so he could over breakfast, but as he sat down at the kitchen table, he heard Shea calling a cheerful greeting to the hands, and then she appeared in the doorway of the kitchen.

"Good morning, bro, Kaden! Mmmm, smells good." She sank gracefully down in the chair beside Logan, and smiled at Kaden. "So did you survive that storm last night?"

Kaden almost choked on a bite of toast, coughing to clear his throat and taking a sip of his orange juice to ease the crumbs down. His voice strained, he replied, "I survived it… okay." Another flush crept up his neck to invade his cheeks.

Logan hid a smile behind his glass of orange juice, but couldn't quite keep the smile off his face as he ate, sneaking little glances at Kaden. At one point, he caught Kaden looking at him, and he winked, almost laughing out loud at the way Kaden's eyes immediately dropped to his plate and the embarrassed expression that graced his features. The younger man was absolutely adorable, and he couldn't wait to have a few moments alone with him again.

Unbeknownst to the two of them, Shea spent most of breakfast observing the glances they shared. She could sense something had changed between them, and as soon as Logan and the men left for the fields, she pounced. "So, Kaden, want to tell me what's goin' on between you and my brother?"

Her abrupt question shocked him so much that he dropped one of the plates he carried, watching in dismay as it smashed to the floor and pieces of glass went everywhere. "I... I... don't know what you mean." He put the rest of the plates in the sink and returned to start picking up the pieces.

Shea leaned back in her chair, a knowing smirk on her rosy lips. "Sure you do. I mean after all, anyone with enough brains could see the looks this morning between you two. Did he kiss you?"

"Eh?!" Kaden winced as a piece of glass wedged itself in his palm due to his being distracted by her words. Pulling it out carefully, he grimaced at the sight of the blood welling up and spilling down his wrist.

"Now look what you made me do!" He glared at her and stood, dumping the pieces of the plate in the trash, and stuck his hand underneath the water running from the faucet, filling the sink. He watched the blood stain the water pink and wondered what he should tell Shea.

Shea stood up and moved to his side. "If you tell me what happened last night, I'll go get you a BAND-AID," she teased, studying the red-faced teenager.

"I... don't like thunderstorms. They... scare me. I guess he heard me last night and came down to check on me. He... we... kissed." He looked down into the soapy water, waiting for her to

92

be disgusted, but to his complete surprise she squealed happily and side-hugged him tightly.

"Finally! I can't believe how long you two have been dancing around the issue!" Shea practically bounced off the floor with her giddiness.

"You... aren't disgusted?" he asked incredulously, turning his head to look at her, his eyes slightly wide.

"Of course not! Why would I be? Because you're two guys? Please. Love comes in all forms, honey. There's no difference between a man and a woman, two men, or two women. I'm so happy! It's the first time I've seen Logan look happy since our parents...." She trailed off and looked away, down at the floor.

Even though curiosity about their parents stung Kaden, he held his tongue, knowing it wasn't right for him to ask when he wasn't exactly forthcoming about his own past. He smiled encouragingly at her and leaned into her hug. "As long as you are okay with it, then I won't worry what others think, I guess. I still don't know if he's okay with what happened."

He looked uncertainly at her, his own concerns and worries obvious in his eyes. "Maybe it was a one-time thing, and he won't want to repeat it. Maybe he did it to try and calm me down since I freaked out about the storm. I don't know." He sighed and pulled away from her to finish getting the dishes from the dining room.

Shea followed to help him, and tried to soothe his fears. "Logan likes you, Kaden. I could see it that first week you were here. Yesterday really upset him when you left. I know it. Besides, if he does anything to upset you, he knows I'll kick his ass." She winked at him, causing him to laugh, his eyes crinkling at the corners.

He finished washing up the dishes, drying them, and putting them away for the next meal. Shea went upstairs to get the BAND-

AID for his palm, and insisted on rubbing it with alcohol, which stung, and then applied the BAND-AID herself. He noticed the way she glanced at his wrist to check if he'd stopped cutting himself. He'd only done it once since the day he'd been in Logan's bathroom. About a week after the incident at the pond, he'd been overcome by memories of his past and his lust for Logan, sending him over the edge. But as he'd watched the blood well up from the first cut, he remembered the promise he'd made to Logan and Shea. Unwilling to ruin the friendship they were building, he'd stopped, dropping the razor into the bathroom sink, watching the blood staining the white porcelain pink. He'd worn the wristband for a while longer, just until that cut had healed enough to where it didn't look fresh. Then he'd removed it and left it off ever since.

After cleaning up the dishes from breakfast, he wandered outside to spend time with Mantacor. Shea left to go see some friends in town, and he waved goodbye, chuckling when Mantacor bumped his shoulder with his nose to get Kaden's attention on him. The horse lapped at his hair, and Kaden wondered if the horse would let him in the corral with him. Maybe it would be all right since Logan suggested that he help him with Mantacor. So he moved over to the gate, opening it and slipping inside before latching it again. Mantacor backed away, and Kaden's expression dropped. Instead of giving up like he would have in the past, he just knelt down where he stood and waited for Mantacor to approach him. The horse continued to shy away from him, coming close only to dart away if Kaden even flicked an eyelash.

Kaden lost all sense of time, concentrating only on the horse, waiting for him to show the trust they'd built together. Mantacor studied him from the middle of the paddock, and after what seemed forever, he slowly moved toward Kaden, step by step, until he stood in front of the boy. Kaden held up his hand and smiled when Mantacor's nose dropped into his palm. "That's a good boy, Mantacor. See, I would never hurt you."

He wrinkled his nose as Mantacor nuzzled his neck where he kneeled, tickling him, and he laughed, startling the horse for a split second before it relaxed again. The sound of trucks and hooves plodding along brought his head up, and he spotted the men heading back to the ranch. That must mean they were bringing back some of the cattle to brand or castrate again. Mantacor heard the sounds and snorted nervously, shifting his hooves against the packed dirt beneath them. Kaden slowly stood up, patting Mantacor's neck gently before turning to leave the paddock. To his astonishment, the horse grabbed the hem of his shirt and tugged, trying to keep him in the paddock. Kaden laughed and turned his head to peer over his shoulder.

"It's all right, Mantacor, I'll come back." But the horse stubbornly refused to let go and started pulling him back into the middle of the corral.

Not knowing what else to do, Kaden followed, and that's where he stood when Logan climbed down from his truck. "Kaden," he called in confusion, coming close to the corral.

"He won't let me out," Kaden explained, feeling a little uncomfortable with the fact that the ranch hands were all standing around staring at him.

Logan felt fear when he saw the nervousness radiating from the horse, and he moved toward the paddock, trying to think of a way to get Kaden out of there. He'd yell at him for entering the corral later. Right now, fear and panic coursed through his veins when he saw that whenever Kaden tried to leave the corral, the horse would push him back. What the hell was that danged horse doing? Then it hit him. Mantacor didn't want to allow Kaden out because he thought they were going to hurt him. Damn, that kid really had accomplished more with that horse than he had in a year.

"Kaden, listen, I think he believes we're going to harm you."

Try to talk him down, and as you do that, move toward the gate." Turning, Logan motioned for his men to go about putting the cattle in the other corrals, and then swung back around to see Kaden crooning softly to the horse, lightly trailing his hands over the horse's muzzle and neck.

Kaden couldn't believe that Mantacor felt the need to protect him. "Hey, buddy, you don't have to protect me, you know. Logan would never hurt me." His voice trailed off for a split second as he realized that a phrase had never been truer. "I need to go, but I promise to come back."

He slowly inched his way backward, still patting Mantacor and whispering soothingly to him. It felt like another hour before he reached the gate, and the horse finally let him go, giving a neigh of fear as he saw Kaden leaving the paddock and the large cowboy coming up beside him. Kaden smiled at the horse and took another sugar cube from his pocket to feed to him. "See, it's all right. I'll be fine, and I'll come back in a little while."

Logan almost slumped to the ground with relief. "What were you thinking?" he demanded, his eyes flashing dangerously.

"I have to earn his complete trust, Logan. You have to understand that. It's not about want; it's what I have to do." Kaden locked his gaze with Logan's, pleading for the older man to understand. He saw the reluctant admiration in the man's eyes, and the way the fight seemed to drain out of him.

"Just don't do that again unless someone is out here with you. You don't know what he would have done," Logan said sternly, his heart finally beginning to settle down after pounding with terror.

Logan waited impatiently until the men had sat down to lunch, and the two of them were in the kitchen, to express his emotions. Kaden stood at the counter, putting together a meal for Logan and himself, when he walked up behind the boy, sliding his

96

hands around the thin waist and resting his chin on Kaden's shoulder. "Don't ever scare me like that again. I don't think my heart could take it," he whispered, his eyes closing as he remembered seeing the teenager in the corral and cornered by the most dangerous horse he'd ever met.

"He would never hurt me." Kaden hesitated for a split second before adding, "Just like I know you'd never hurt me, Logan."

Affection and another emotion he couldn't define flooded Logan. He moved his head up to press his lips close to Kaden's ear. "I wanted to kiss you again so badly this morning. I couldn't think of anything but that while we were heading back in. My only fear is that you regret that it happened."

"Never," Kaden said fiercely, leaning back into Logan's embrace, and he felt the arms around him tighten for a fraction of a second.

"I actually wondered the same thing about you," Kaden admitted a moment later. "That you would regret it, or it had only been a way to distract me from my fears."

"No matter how afraid someone was, I would never kiss someone unless I wanted to." Logan had been just about to spin him around to take the kiss he wanted when they heard the sounds of chairs scraping against the floor in the dining room, and he pulled away reluctantly.

"I'll just take it with me to eat outside. I'll see you tonight, Kaden." Logan quickly wrapped up his lunch and headed back out to join his men, frustration eating away at his patience, and he snapped at the first man who made a mistake.

CHAPTER 9

KADEN spent the rest of the afternoon on cloud nine, a wide grin spreading across his face, flushed in pleasure. While listening to the sounds of the men shouting and the cattle fussing about being branded, he made up chicken parmigiana and fettuccini Alfredo for the dinner meal, setting up the dining room and kitchen in a nice layout. Shea came home a short while before dinner, helping wherever he needed. She kept hounding him to tell her what had him so happy, but he wanted to keep it secret, held to his heart, the ice slowly melting away. So he kept his mouth shut and would just smile that mysterious, I-know-something-you-don't smile. It drove her to toss her hands up in the air and let out a frustrated growl. "Fine. Don't tell me. Meanie."

With that, she darted up the stairs to change. Kaden shivered in anticipation when he heard the sounds of men laughing and boots crunching along the ground. His horse-riding lessons had advanced far enough to where he could saddle a horse on his own, and even go riding if he wanted to by himself. He preferred to wait until Logan or Shea could accompany him, though. Plus, he didn't really know too much about the ranch just yet, so it wouldn't do to get lost. He'd only serve to cause problems for them. It felt so good to have something that had lasted longer than a week, and to know that Logan wanted him to stay on even after the job was over.

His writing had taken a turn from a sense of dreaming for something he could never have to a more upbeat "I have what I want" in the last couple of weeks. He was still uncertain about showing or telling Logan or Shea about his writing. It was so personal, and it would open the door to his mind and soul. Showing them the truth of whom and what he is. He wasn't sure if he was ready for that, or if he would ever be. But it might be the last step toward showing them that he trusted them. His fingers traced over the scars on his wrist, and he wondered if his mind could handle reliving those memories enough to tell his story to Logan and Shea. It would be the first time since he'd been fifteen that he'd contemplated talking about his past with someone. If he did let Logan know his secrets, would Logan be disgusted with him? Would he want to touch him after he told him all the horrific details? Those thoughts brought him to a blinding halt, and his lips twisted bitterly. He'd probably go running as fast and as far as his long, muscular legs could take him. And Kaden would never be able to blame Logan, because he wasn't clean or innocent like Logan believed him to be.

His thoughts were interrupted when he heard someone enter the kitchen. Schooling his features into a bland mask, he turned to find Logan leaning against the doorjamb, just watching him. His heart thudded painfully in his chest as he pictured that soft smiling expression changing to one of horror and disgust. Would he be able to handle watching that happen? His eyes stung slightly, and he swung back around to face the sink, finishing up washing some of the dishes he'd used to prepare the dinner meal. He didn't want Logan to realize he'd begun to cry.

"Is something wrong, Kaden?" That deep, husky voice drizzled over his ears like sweet caramel over ice cream, sending a shiver of pleasure down his spine.

"I'm fine. Just a little tired. Is everyone enjoying the meal?"

Kaden bent his head slightly, partially shielding his features from Logan.

"Mmm. They seem to be. I thought I'd eat in here with you again. If you don't mind, that is." Logan moved closer, sensing Kaden hadn't been entirely truthful, but he didn't know how to get Kaden to open up to him.

"Of course. It's your house, right?"

"What's that supposed to mean?" Logan demanded, straightening his body and stepping closer to Kaden, leaning against the sink.

"N... nothing. I just...." Kaden swallowed painfully hard, realizing that it probably sounded like he didn't want Logan there. Forcing himself to smile, knowing that it merely trembled on his lips, he turned to Logan. "I'm sorry. I didn't mean it like that. I didn't go back to sleep last night, and I'm just tired."

It must have worked, because Logan's features softened, and an affectionate gleam invaded those beautiful green pools of his. Kaden's eyes slid closed as Logan brushed two fingers over his unmarred cheek, caressing him gently. "It's all right. I didn't sleep, either."

Kaden leaned into the caress, feeling his throat tighten with unshed tears, and he wondered again if Logan would be so willing to touch him if Kaden told him how disgusting he truly was.

"I'm sure you're hungry. Sit." Kaden opened his eyes, smiling up at Logan, unaware that the smile didn't quite reach his eyes or noticing the way that Logan's eyes narrowed a tiny bit at the edges, taking in the weary look on the teen's face.

"Sit with me. Tell me what you did today. Besides enter Mantacor's corral," the cowboy reprimanded without any heat behind it.

Kaden settled into the seat beside Logan, going through the

motions of eating, and gave him a brief rundown of what he'd done that day. The moment their plates were clear, Kaden stood up from his seat to start doing dishes. He could hear the men in the dining room also finishing up. Gratefully, he started the water to fill the sink, adding soap, and then Kaden started carting dishes from the dining room to the kitchen sink. Logan didn't say much, just stood up and started helping him before taking up station beside him to dry them. They worked in companionable silence until the task was completed, and then Logan gently took Kaden's hand, drawing him close to his chest. He tipped Kaden's chin up with one finger and searched the boy's eyes with his own. "No matter what's happened to you in the past or what you've done to survive, I could never judge you for anyone other than who you are right now. You do know that, don't you, Kaden?"

Kaden's eyes widened at how intuitively Logan picked up on his thoughts, and he let out a small breath of air in surprise. Before he could respond, Logan's lips claimed his in the kiss that the cowboy had been waiting for all day. They moved softly, seductively over Kaden's, shifting like they had a mind of their own. Kaden felt Logan's tongue questing for entrance to his mouth, and with a slight sigh of pleasure, he granted it, his body shuddering when Logan pushed inside. Their tongues slid slickly over one another, dancing and undulating, pressing close and drawing back, only to push close again.

Logan groaned low in his chest at the feel of the soft, moist flesh his mouth dominated. The kid tasted like cinnamon, and spices, clean and fresh, all rolled into one. Nothing existed except this feeling, nothing but the two of them together—touching, caressing, their mouths locked together in mimic of another more primeval act. Logan felt his body hardening and moaned. Not wanting to frighten the younger man, he stopped, unlocking his mouth from Kaden's to lean his forehead against his.

"You have no idea what you do to me. I know something is bothering you, and I may not have gained your trust one hundred percent yet, but when you're ready to talk, I'm here to listen. Good night, my little one." He drew out the last sentence, savoring the feel of the endearment on his tongue before he disentangled himself from Kaden. And without turning back, because turning back would only send him straight into the other man's arms, he strode from the kitchen and directly up to his own bathroom to take a cold shower.

The next morning, Kaden groggily slapped the alarm off and groaned as he rolled out of bed. He'd only just fallen asleep, the words Logan had uttered the night before leaving him breathless and sleepless. Could he trust Logan to that depth? Rubbing his eyes, he yawned as he made his way to the bathroom to brush his teeth and hair. As he ran the toothbrush over his molars, he stared at his sleep-deprived features in the mirror and pictured the moment between them last night. The kiss could only be defined as erotic and amazing, but at the same time, too good to be true. The feel of Logan's lips on his had been more exquisite than anything he had ever felt in his life. Sighing, he spit the toothpaste into the sink, rinsed his mouth out with water, and wiped his mouth with a small hand towel lying on the bathroom counter.

He dressed in his usual clothing, studying himself in the mirror that hung on the back of the closet door, and wondered what the big cowboy saw in a scrawny little nobody like him. His eyes, as always, were shadowed with the horrors from his past, his skin having tanned slightly in certain places from his horseback riding lessons, and he slowly lifted his shirt up to look at the various scars and marks all over his chest and belly. Similar ones ran the length of his back and arms. They were different sizes and shapes. A knife here, a cigarette there, a razor blade across his soft stomach, the tip of a knife heated to the point of glowing pressed against his nipples, leaving them puckered and ugly. He almost sobbed at the thought of showing someone as beautiful as Logan his repulsive form.

Yanking his shirt back down roughly, Kaden slammed the

closet door shut and ran down the hall to the kitchen, the demons of his past on the edge of his heels. Halfway through breakfast, he heard Logan's boots on the stairs. He tried to school his features so he wouldn't appear upset, but by the look Logan gave him, it wasn't very successful. "Good morning, Kaden," Logan bid as he entered the kitchen.

"Good morn—" His words were cut off by the soft, yet firm, lips crushing against his, and he was dragged, flour-covered hands and all, up against Logan's broad chest. His head whirled with the feelings raging through him, and if Logan hadn't been supporting him where he stood, he would have crumpled to the ground when he felt that wonderfully wet, incredibly slick tongue brush over his bottom lip, seeking entrance, which he gladly granted with a soft moan.

Logan pulled away, gasping for breath, and smiled softly down at Kaden, running his fingers through the dark hair on his right temple. "Mmm. Now, I could wake up that way every morning." He dropped a light kiss on the tip of Kaden's nose before setting him away from him and turning to pour himself a cup of fresh coffee.

Kaden's breathing was slightly heavy, and he turned back to preparing the pancake batter in a daze. His body tingled everywhere, and that was only from a kiss. What would it be like if he were to actually touch him everywhere? Immediately, he felt overpowered by the same violent sensation of lust being wrong, shameful. The urge to cut weighed on him, and he gritted his teeth, gripping the counter hard. He breathed deeply, trying to keep from letting it overtake him. "Kaden? What's wrong?" He heard Logan's voice over the angry buzz in his head, and tried to smile reassuringly, but it only made it to a grimace before it slipped away.

"I... it's... no... nothing," Kaden gasped, shaking his head.

"It's obviously something! Or you wouldn't be so freaked

out."

"I'll ex... explain it la... later." Kaden closed his eyes and bent his head down toward the sink, turning the water on full blast, and shoved his head under the water, ignoring the gasp of surprise from Logan. The cold water sluiced over his head, drenching his dark hair and causing it to fall around his face like a wet curtain. His mind began to clear, and he started to breathe a little easier. When he turned the water off, he jumped when he felt Logan place a towel over his head and begin to dry his hair, his strong fingers massaging his scalp at the same time. He stifled a groan at the feel of Logan's body lightly leaning against his side and tried to stay relaxed while the cowboy dried his hair. "Th-thank you," he stuttered once Logan had finished.

"You're welcome. Someday you'll have to tell me what that was all about," Logan commented as he laid the towel over the back of a chair to dry before picking up his coffee again, sipping at it while watching Kaden from beneath hooded eyes.

Kaden finger-combed his hair and got back to finishing up breakfast, barely managing to have it on the table by the time everyone arrived. He wasn't really hungry after the storm of emotions that had run through him and just started washing the dishes that he'd used to make breakfast.

Logan sat at the table, eating slowly, still contemplating Kaden and trying to puzzle out what had just happened this morning. "You aren't going to eat?" he questioned the teenager.

"I'm not really hungry right now. I'll get something later, when I am."

Logan could see that in the almost two months that the teenager had been on the ranch, he'd gained a small amount of weight. Enough to where his body had started to fill out in certain areas. It made him feel good to see that, and he hoped that Kaden wouldn't revert back to not eating. After finishing up his meal, he stood to place his plate on the side of the kitchen sink. "We'll be in around the same time as always. Stay out of Mantacor's corral, Kaden. I mean it." He gave Kaden a stern look, reaching out to lightly touch the pale skin of Kaden's smooth cheek.

"I promise," Kaden replied, giving him a tired smile.

"Good. I'll see you at lunchtime, then." Logan left, barking at his men to hurry up and finish so they could get started. They would remain at the ranch again today with more cattle to brand before transporting them back out on the range.

Kaden tried not to analyze the things that had happened or think about how he'd almost lost it in front of Logan. That had left a vile taste in the back of his throat. What would have happened if he hadn't succeeded? It would have left Logan disgusted, for sure, to see him so desperately trying to ease the pain in his heart by causing physical pain on his body. Someone had once told him, a psychiatrist he'd been forced to see after—he shut that door in his mind quickly. She had told him that it was a way that the mind found to release its pain in a more physical form, and that even though you are hurting yourself, it shows that you are desperately trying to cling to life. In some ways it's better because it shows that you aren't totally ready to give up on life yet. She'd told him that he needed to learn to control it, to control himself, one day at a time. Since that day at the pond, he'd only done it once, because every time he'd picked up a razor or knife thereafter, he saw Shea and Logan's face that day, pleading with him not to do it. He hadn't wanted to disappoint them, so he'd managed to control it, but how long would it be before he did it again?

The dishes didn't take long, and then he was outside in the early sunshine to visit Mantacor. This time he stayed out of the corral and just patted and spoke to him while the horse munched on the treats he'd brought with him. "Sometimes I wonder why I didn't kill myself that night, too, Mantacor. It would have eased the world of a burden like me. And I wouldn't be here, causing trouble for Logan and Shea."

Kaden laughed lightly as Mantacor nuzzled at his neck, tickling the hair at the base. "Well, at least I know you care about me, huh? Thank you for yesterday, boy. I understand what you were trying to do, and I haven't felt that safe in a very long time."

Unaware of the ears nearby that were listening, Kaden stayed there with Mantacor for a while longer. Before heading back inside, he promised the horse to come back again later. Shea stepped out of the shadows of the barn and watched him walking into the house, her green eyes sad at having heard his words. The first thing he'd said had registered in her mind, and she wondered what he had meant by that. Had Kaden killed someone? Was that what caused that deep wound in his soul? Shea spun on the heel of her boot and dashed to the corral where the cattle were kept before being either shipped for sale or herded back out onto the range. She needed to speak to her brother. The depth of despair in Kaden's voice had disturbed her greatly. Something had obviously happened to trigger his depression, and she wondered if that something had to do with Logan.

Kaden had just poured himself a glass of lemonade when he heard the sound of men approaching outside. He grinned at the familiar noise and waited anxiously to see Logan. He noticed something off as soon as Logan came into the house, from the way the man wouldn't look at him, and the way he chose to sit in the dining room with the ranch hands instead of with Kaden like he always did. His heart wrenched in his chest, and he wondered what had happened between that morning and now. The appetite that had only returned that morning fled, and he escaped down the hall to his bedroom, closing the door with a soft click behind him. He leaned against it, swallowing convulsively to keep from sobbing. The unshed tears built up behind his eyes, and his head started to pound with tension. He closed his eyes, slumping down to the ground, and cradled his head in his palms. His eyes burned as he sat there trying to keep from falling apart.

Eventually, the sounds of men talking, silverware hitting dishes and chairs scraping the floor faded as the hands returned to their work. He slowly dragged himself up and went out into the kitchen to begin cleaning up and preparing the dinner meal. His back was stiff as he worked, and he became so lost in his despair that he didn't hear Shea enter the room behind him.

"Kaden?" she queried softly, studying his dejected form.

Kaden jumped, but only slightly, and he gazed at her, eyes dull. "Hey, Shea."

"What's wrong?" she exclaimed, her stomach clenching at the pained expression in Kaden's eyes.

"Nothing's wrong. I'm just tired. Did you need something?" Kaden swung back to the sink to continue washing dishes, hardly seeing what he was really doing, just going through the motions.

Shea didn't understand why Kaden seemed as though the world had suddenly fallen onto his shoulders, and decided to let it be for now. When he wanted to talk, he'd tell her. "No, I didn't need anything, Kaden. I'm going out for a while, I'll be back later." She turned and left, headed into town to see her friend.

After making sure that everything had been prepared to cook the dinnertime meal, Kaden went back into his bedroom, shutting the door behind him and locking it. He lay across the bed, his heart thudding painfully in his chest. What had he done? His fingers clenched in the sheets around him as he tried to control his desire to cut. The urge clawed at him, devouring his self-control, demanding and taunting him. He could hear the voice in his head telling him to do it, to stop the pain in his heart. Reaching into the nightstand beside the bed, he withdrew the small penknife he had, staring at it as the silver blade flashed in the light from the window. He sat up, his back against the headboard, and lowered the blade to his wrist, making a small incision, watching the blood well up, beading on his skin and beginning to spill over. Small drops landed on his bed sheets, but he ignored them, making another small cut, and another, and another.

Relief, blessed relief, flooded his heart, and he closed his eyes, breathing in and out softly. He lay there, crimson spreading across the leg of his jeans and the sheet beneath him, as the physical pain chased away the emotional ache. The world around him faded into nothing, his eyes opening but not really seeing the white walls around him. The sounds of someone coming into the house brought him out of the euphoric trance that he'd fallen into, and he scrambled off the bed, dropping the penknife on the floor in his haste to get to the bathroom to rinse off the blood. Shame at his lack of control devastated him, and hot tears trickled from his eyes, trailing down his cheeks as he washed his arm before wrapping it in gauze. He went back out into the bedroom to his closet to dig out the wristband from his duffel bag, where he'd stuffed it after taking it off last time. He knew they would know. The band snapped into place with a resounding clunk, almost like a shackle. He quickly threw on another pair of jeans, stuffing the stained ones into his bag.

Kaden stripped the sheets from his bed, wincing at how the blood had stained through to the mattress. The blankets were in the hall closet just outside his door, and he cautiously opened it, peering out to see if whoever had entered the house had left yet. Hearing no noises, he slipped out and hurriedly grabbed the first available sheets, sneaking back into his room and shutting the door again. He made short work of making the bed, and stood there, his lungs laboring from the panic setting in. What had he done? He saw the penknife on the floor and slowly bent over to pick it up, wincing at the red that stained the blade. He carefully placed it in the nightstand, shutting the drawer as quietly as possible, as though making any sound would shatter him.

CHAPTER 10

"OH, KADEN, you didn't!" he heard Shea exclaim behind him as he stood at the kitchen sink, wincing at her words and knowing what she meant.

He gripped the edge of the sink, hard. "I told you I'd try, Shea. I'm sorry." His voice came out rough, and he tensed when he felt her arms slide around his waist from behind and her forehead lean against his back.

"Why, Kaden?"

"The physical pain hurts less than the emotional pain." He repeated the words he'd used at the pond.

They stood there for what could have been minutes or even hours, both unaware of the passage of time. Finally, Kaden couldn't stop himself from asking, "Shea... did I do something to upset Logan?" An uncertain tone entered his voice.

"No. Of course not, Kaden. Why would you think that?" Shea asked in bewilderment. "Is that why you cut yourself? Because you think he's upset with you?"

Kaden gave a small nod, looking down into the sink. "He... wouldn't even... look at me at lunch. He... normally sits with me. I...." His voice caught in his throat, and he stopped speaking.

"Oh, Kaden." She couldn't believe her stupid, pig-headed brother would be so insensitive. Logan had overreacted yet again. "I'll talk to Logan and find out what's going on."

"No!" He panicked, pushing away from her. "No. Don't. It's fine. If he… regrets anything, then I have to live with that. It's fine. I'll go back to New York when the three months are up, and I'll be fine." Instantly, Kaden knew he'd just lied to Shea. His life would never be the same again. Logan had done something no one else ever had. The big, gentle cowboy had reached inside him and jump-started his heart again. Leaving Logan would mean leaving a huge part of himself here.

"Don't talk like that. Logan invited you to stay here, and that's what you're going to do." Shea glared at him, her hands on her hips.

He gave her a weak smile at the way she looked standing there, her hair wild around her face and her eyes flashing angrily, a stubborn expression on her face. "We'll see, Shea. Please don't tell Logan about this." He pointed at his wrist. "I am just going to go into my room until everyone finishes eating. I can't take being yelled at right now. And I'm sure he will, that is if he still cares enough to."

"He cares," Shea protested, but Kaden just sadly shook his head and went back to finishing up the dinner preparations.

Kaden did as he had told Shea, disappearing into his bedroom until he heard the last man leave and Logan's boots on the stairs. The lights were out when he left his room, and he flicked on the one in the kitchen, starting the hot water up to fill the sink. He trudged back and forth between the dining room and the kitchen, placing the plates on the counter. In the middle of washing, he heard a noise behind him, he turned his head slightly to see Logan standing in the doorway in nothing but a pair of jeans, his sandy blond hair damp from his shower. Tensing, he turned his head back to the dishes, trying to keep his wrist from view. He had no idea how long the man had stood there, so he couldn't be sure if Logan had already seen it or not.

Logan watched the boy's thin back, not knowing what to say or how to apologize for hurting him like that. Shea had taken a chunk out of his hide, dragging him out of earshot of the ranch hands to give him a piece of her mind. She had told him about how Kaden had cut himself again because of his actions, and that Kaden had been so upset he'd spoken of leaving at the end of the three months. He knew he'd overreacted about what Shea told him the teenager had said to the horse. He'd been hurt, angry, and just plain frustrated. He wanted so badly for Kaden to trust him, and to open himself up to him, but he kept butting up against a brick wall, unable to break through and reach Kaden. But he'd never wanted to hurt him, ever. "Kaden, I—" He stopped, still not knowing what to say.

Kaden remained silent. The only sound in the room was the clatter of dishes as he washed and rinsed them, setting them in the rack to air-dry until he finished washing all of them. It remained the same until he pulled the plug from the sink, reaching for the towel to dry them. He'd just reached for the first dish when he felt Logan's hands come down on his shoulders. He flinched, even though he tried to stop himself. Then those hands slid down and around his body, pulling him against the planes of Logan's hard body. Logan buried his face in Kaden's hair, and pleaded, "I'm sorry, Kaden. Please forgive me. I didn't mean to hurt you. I'm so sorry."

Astonishment washed over Kaden, and he couldn't speak. He didn't know what to say, and he felt Logan shudder behind him. "I made a mistake, and I'm sorry. I know that the way I treated you today was unforgivable, and I have no right to ask for your forgiveness, but please, Kaden. I… don't want to lose you." Kaden jerked in surprise at the last part of Logan's sentence.

He leaned back into Logan's warm embrace and set the dish

towel on the counter before turning around in Logan's arms. He reached up and wrapped his arms around Logan's neck and hugged him tightly, resting his cheek against Logan's chest. He felt the big man's breath ruffling the hair on his head and the way Logan's strong arms flexed, surrounding him, pulling him harder against the cowboy.

Logan backed up, drawing Kaden with him until the back of his knees hit the chair behind him. He sat, bringing Kaden down into his lap without breaking the hold they had on one another. They sat like that in silence, no words exchanged, just embracing one another. Logan felt so guilty and ashamed of himself. He should have known better. He knew he had to explain why he reacted that way, and he started quietly, "Kaden?"

Kaden pulled back to look up at Logan in question and waited for the cowboy to speak. "I… want to tell you about our parents. I realized something this afternoon. That in order to gain your trust, I have to show you that you already have mine."

The violet eyes looking so seriously up at him made Logan feel yet again ashamed of his overreaction to what Shea had told him this morning. "Since I can remember, my parents always fought. Constantly. Over every little thing in the world that they could find."

"Bu… but they look so happy in those photos on the stairs!" Kaden couldn't resist interrupting in shock.

Logan's lips twisted in a bitter smile, and he answered the obvious question in Kaden's words, "Appearances can be deceiving, Kaden. They showed an outward appearance of being a loving, caring couple. They're the whole reason I made the decision to never marry. I'm hoping that Shea will decide for herself to marry that big lug Ty. But I can't force her to. Anyway, for years, I always believed that's how all families were. Smiling and happy in public, but at home, yelling and screaming. My father never hit my mother or even us kids, but the yelling scared the hell out of me and Shea. Sometimes I think he wanted to hit my mom but he couldn't bring himself to."

Kaden rested his head against Logan's shoulder as the man spoke, breathing in the scent of his shampoo, and the fragrant soap on his skin. One hand lay trapped between their bodies and the other came up to rest against his broad chest as it rumbled with Logan's words. It made him sad to hear that Logan's parents really weren't as happy as they seemed in the pictures on the stairs. He'd thought that Logan had been so lucky to be blessed with such a wonderful family.

"At that time, my dad owned the local garage, so we lived in town instead of out here. Several times the neighbors called in the sheriff, but without actual physical abuse there wasn't anything he could do to stop it. The fighting eventually stopped, just after I turned eighteen. I came home from school to find my mother and father dead. Apparently, my father had shot her, and then turned the gun on himself in his grief at what he'd done."

A gasp ripped from Kaden's throat, and he reared back to gaze in horror at Logan. He lifted his hand to rest it against Logan's cheek. "I'm so sorry." His breath rushed out of him with a small squeak when Logan squeezed him tightly, burying his face in the side of Kaden's neck.

"It's all right. Both Shea and I have come to accept it as best we could, and we've managed to move on with our lives in most ways. My parents left us well-provided for because of my mother's life insurance policy, and we sold the garage. Neither of us wanted it. We both agreed to buy this ranch and make a go of it. It's grown and prospered a lot since then." Logan hesitated for only a split second before adding, "And now I have you," the last whispered against the skin of Kaden's throat. Logan couldn't stop himself from pressing his lips over the pulse beating at the base of his neck, feeling Kaden shudder in his arms.

Kaden stroked Logan's hair, the words uttered just seconds

ago resounding in his head. Would Logan think that if he knew the truth about him? Logan pulled back to smile down at him. "I am truly sorry for what I put you through today. I didn't mean to hurt you like that. I should have known better. Even though it's no excuse, my only reason for my actions is because Shea overheard you talking to Mantacor. Telling him that no one else cared about you, and that you wished you had killed yourself. I felt... hurt and angry that you didn't understand how much I care about you."

When Kaden heard Logan explain to him that Shea had overheard his words to Mantacor, he'd thought she'd understood everything he'd said, but from what the way that Logan said it, it didn't appear to be so. Now he felt guilty for hurting Logan, and he leaned up to kiss Logan softly, hesitantly, waiting to see if Logan would return it. He almost fainted from relief when Logan kissed him back, their lips moving over each other in a tender caress.

"I'm sorry, Logan. I do understand that you care about me. You've never treated me any other way than with kindness and affection. And"—he looked down at his hands—"I don't want you to be upset, but right now, talking about my past hurts. I promise that when I feel I am ready, I will tell you, but... I'm so afraid that once you know everything about me, you won't want me anymore." His voice lowered to a mere hum of sound as he continued, and Logan almost didn't hear the latter part of his sentence.

"I don't care if you're a convict on the run from the law, or you steal cars for a living, or you were a high-paid escort in your past, Kaden. You're beautiful as you are, and all of that is your past, not your present, or your future." Logan cupped Kaden's cheek, forcing his eyes to meet his. "I like you for you, Kaden. Everything before isn't what you are. It's what has made you who you are."

He paused, wondering if he should say it, but he couldn't seem to stop himself from uttering his next words. "And I think

I'm falling in love with you."

Kaden's eyes widened, and his body stiffened. What had he just said? "I... I...." He didn't know what to say or how to respond. Did he feel that way about Logan? Could he ever be free from his past to be able to love him like he deserved?

Logan let out a small laugh, and ran the thumb of his hand still cupping Kaden's cheek over his skin in a caress. "It's all right. You don't have to respond right now. I understand if you can't bring yourself to feel the same way. But I won't stop from trying to capture your heart." The last was said with such confidence that it sounded like a promise.

Before Kaden could say another word, Logan kissed him again, and again, leaving him senseless and breathless when he set him in one of the empty kitchen chairs. Logan's chest heaved with each breath he pulled into his lungs and there were drops of sweat on his forehead. When the cowboy stood, Kaden flushed bright red, his face lighting up like a Christmas tree, when his eyes narrowed in on the obvious bulge in Logan's jeans. Logan smirked and leaned over to drop a kiss on top of Kaden's head. "Good night, little one. I'll see you in the morning. Get some sleep, okay?" Kaden nodded dumbly in response.

The large cowboy strode from the room, leaving Kaden in the kitchen with his thoughts. Could he accept what Logan had told him? Would he really still care for him once Kaden told him about the blood he had on his hands and the things that he had done? He dropped his head into his hands and stifled a sob, his body shuddering with the effort. How do you reveal to someone that you're a murderer? Do you just walk up to them and say hey guess what? I killed somebody. Sighing, he wearily pushed himself up from the chair and walked out of the kitchen, flipping the light switch off as he passed by.

Strong hands held him down, pain searing through him as the hot knife edge pressed against his flesh, ripping screams of agony from his throat. Tears streamed down his face, his body convulsing in pain. "Please, No!"

"Did you think I wouldn't notice?! Did you? I saw the way you looked at that other man. You're nothing but a whore!" He felt the man's breath, heavy with alcohol, sliding across his skin, and he gagged, scrambling frantically to get away.

Numbness washed over him as he felt his clothes being torn from his body, and the sounds of a belt being unbuckled and a zipper lowering reached his ears. His legs were pushed open wide and high above his head as his violator rammed the blunt column of flesh into him, tearing his sensitive flesh. Blood spilled down to pool beneath his body, and he fell into the blessed oblivion of unconsciousness.

Kaden sat up, screams of terror coming from him, his hands flailing blindly in the darkness before him. Salty tears rained down from his eyes, panic shining from them. He barely registered the pounding on his bedroom door, and then it burst open, Logan having thrown his body against it.

The doorjamb splintered, but Logan didn't give a damn as he saw Kaden sitting there, still screaming. He sprinted toward the bed and gripped Kaden's shaking shoulders. "Kaden? Kaden!" He shook him lightly, trying to get him to stop.

Shea stood in the doorway, her hand over her mouth at the sound of Kaden's terrified wailing, and she stepped up to Kaden, reaching out a hand to slap him lightly on the cheek. His cries cut off abruptly, and he sat there, panting for breath, tears still trailing down his pale cheeks. "L-Logan? Shea?" he stammered, realizing that they were in the room with him.

"Jesus. You almost gave me a heart attack," Logan said

fiercely, gathering him close to his chest for the second time that night. "I don't think I've ever heard such frightful screams before."

"I… I'm sorry," Kaden whispered, his arms coming up around Logan's broad back, gripping the older man tightly. "I'm sorry. I'm sorry," he mumbled over and over again.

"Shhh. It's all right. It was just a nightmare. It's over." Logan motioned for Shea to leave, and once she had left, closing the door as much as possible since it now sat crooked on its hinges, he slid them both into a prone position. He just held the teenager close and listened as the boy's breathing evened out, and eventually Kaden slipped into an exhausted sleep. When he'd heard the sounds coming from downstairs, he'd instantly known that they were coming from Kaden, and his heart had started to pound in panic and fear. He had not known what to expect when he'd entered the room, but to find that it was nothing more than a nightmare that caused such bone-chilling cries, made him wonder even more what the younger man's past held.

"Someday, you'll tell me. Until then, I'll be by your side to keep these nightmares at bay," he murmured against the dark head, knowing that Kaden couldn't hear him.

When the alarm went off at three thirty, Kaden reached out to turn it off, and started with surprise when he realized that he wasn't alone in the bed. He sat up quickly, his eyes zeroing in on Logan's face. What the hell? He searched his memory and remembered the nightmare. He shuddered at the memories, and then realized with awe that Logan had stayed with him throughout the night to keep him safe. Logan stirred and mumbled something in his sleep, causing Kaden's gaze to jump back to his face.

"L-Logan," he called lightly, reaching out a shaky hand to touch the big man's shoulder, shaking him gently. "Logan?"

Logan woke slowly, his eyes opening to find Kaden's dark head bent close to his and his hand on his shoulder. He smiled up at Kaden, and reached out a hand to lightly caress the boy's cheek before yawning and stretching like a sleepy lion. "Time to get up?"

Kaden nodded slowly and watched as Logan slid from the bed, his chest still bare, his long lean legs covered by a pair of jeans that he'd thrown on in his haste to get to Kaden last night. "I... I'm sorry about last night," he apologized into the darkness.

"Don't be. We all have nightmares. Remember what I told you when you first got here." Logan smiled encouragingly at Kaden, and walked around the bed to the door. With a grimace, he said, "I'll have Charlie fix that for you. I kind of... lost it when I couldn't get in last night. Do me a favor. Don't lock your door anymore at night. I don't think my heart can take it. You're going to be the death of me, kid." He smiled to show his words were only a joke, and walked over to pull Kaden out of bed.

"L-Logan, I... uh... want to tell you about my past," Kaden said in a subdued tone, his eyes tilted at the floor, his hand still encased in Logan's larger one. "Tonight. Um... I... just promise me that you won't hate me," he pleaded, lifting his gaze to meet Logan's.

"I already told you last night, Kaden. Nothing you tell me will change the way I feel about you." He smiled down at the teenager, trailing the backs of his fingers over the smooth skin of his cheek. "I'm glad to know that you're willing to trust me. I will be with you, Kaden. And no matter what the future may bring, I won't back down."

Kaden smiled, still uncertain about Logan's reaction. He gave a nod at Logan and carefully extricated his hand from the cowboy's. "Wait, don't I get a good-morning kiss?" Logan pouted, and Kaden's heart skipped a beat at the adorable look.

Laughing, he pushed himself up on his tiptoes and brushed his lips over Logan's, but before he could pull back, Logan's arms clamped around him, and he deepened the kiss. Their tongues

118

brushed erotically over each other, dueling for dominance that Kaden let Logan have after only a moment, moaning into the larger man's mouth. "Now that is a good-morning kiss," Logan whispered when he pulled back, setting Kaden aside and slowly walking from the room.

Kaden stared after the cowboy for a moment, and grinned broadly, happily. He brushed his teeth and washed up quickly, dressing in a pair of faded jeans and a white T-shirt. Breakfast was the usual, quiet affair, as most of the men were still trying to wake up for the day.

Shea gave him a concerned look when she came into the kitchen to get herself a cup of coffee, and he smiled reassuringly at her, happy to see her expression turn to relief and then peace. She ruffled his hair lightly and dropped a kiss on his cheek. "Good morning, Kaden. So do you think you'd want to go horseback riding today? I kind of have the urge to get out there and ride, and thought you might be tired of being cooped up in the house all day."

He nodded eagerly, and they planned to leave as soon as the men headed out. He intended to stop by and see Mantacor first, and then go riding. Logan stopped in to see him one last time before heading out into the fields with the men. Shea forced Kaden to eat, even though he wasn't really hungry, and then he grabbed an apple for Mantacor before following her from the house. She went into the barn to saddle the horses while he stopped to give the white stallion his treat and croon to him for a few moments. "You ready, Kaden?" Shea called from where she stood, holding the reins to two horses.

The sun rose slowly, casting pink and yellow fingers along the horizon as they rode, and Shea chatted about her visits to her friends. Kaden asked her about Ty and asked if she loved him. She admitted that she did, but she didn't know if she could deal with marriage because of her parents. He revealed to her that Logan had told him about their parents, and also what he'd said about her—that he wanted her to marry Ty. Shea didn't believe him at first, but after he'd kept insisting, she relented and believed him. It amazed her that her brother would be so willing for her to get married after everything that happened with their mother and father. She watched Kaden and the way horseback riding made him feel so content. The look of peace on his face told the story of healing taking place inside of him. He might never heal completely on the outside, but perhaps, with time and with the help of people who loved and cared about him, he could heal on the inside enough to live a normal life and not cringe in fear of everyone around him.

"Logan said he wants to set up that punching bag for you and teach you some of the moves so that if you feel the need to cut again, you can do that instead," Shea mentioned casually.

Kaden looked down at the mane of his horse, fondling a few strands in discomfort. "I'm sorry, Shea. I know I promised I wouldn't do it again, but everything became too much. It's like something inside me takes over, and I can't stop it. Like those people who are obsessive-compulsive. I met a few of them when I...." He trailed off and abruptly switched his train of thought. "I think I'd like him to do that for me."

"I'll talk to him at dinner when he gets back. Tomorrow's Sunday, so you guys can work on it then," Shea said happily, bouncing in her saddle slightly.

He wondered sadly if that would be the truth after he told Logan about his past and the things he'd done. Perhaps it would be. Logan had seemed so sincere in his words that morning and last night. He wouldn't know for sure until he told Logan, but he sent a prayer to God, begging Him to let the man's words be true, because this time, he knew there'd be no return from the edge. He could sense it inside him, the weakness. It waited eagerly for the slightest bit of pain to beat at him to cut, to make it deeper and deeper until it wasn't simply cutting. "Sure. That would be great."

CHAPTER 11

THEY headed back as it inched close to 11 a.m. Mantacor let out a neigh of greeting as they approached, and Kaden smiled. Once they'd unsaddled and brushed the horses down, he stopped by to see the white stallion for a brief moment and then headed into the house to start making lunch for him and Shea. Logan surprised Kaden by returning to the house alone for lunch. Once she'd spoken to Logan about the punching bag, Shea disappeared upstairs—with a fabricated excuse—to give the two men some privacy. Logan and Kaden shared lunch in the kitchen, just talking. Kaden asked Logan about the entire roundup process. It turned out that in the next couple of weeks they would be bringing in the last of the cattle and wrapping things up shortly thereafter. Logan explained how and why they castrated the steers which reminded Kaden of those things he'd seen in the grocery store that day. "You… uh… don't eat calf fries, do you?" His expression twisted in disgust.

Logan laughed, and nodded. "Yep. I love 'em. Don't worry. You'll get a chance to try them at the end-of-roundup barbecue that we have every year."

"I don't think so!" Kaden exclaimed, bringing his hand to his mouth to cover it.

"Oh, come on! Where's your sense of adventure?" Logan teased, his lips curved in a wide smile.

"I don't think my sense of adventure reaches quite that far, Logan!" He shook his head, standing up to bring his dish to the sink and reaching for Logan's at the same time. Logan's hand closed over his wrist, the one without the armband, and he ran his thumb over the silky skin there, watching Kaden's eyes darken with pleasure.

Logan's voice sounded husky with need when he spoke next. "I hope it reaches to some points."

A flush ran across Kaden's pale cheeks at the suggestion behind Logan's words, and he swallowed hard. "I... I think it does." The flush deepened at his response, and he dropped his eyes to the table.

Releasing Kaden's wrist, Logan stood, winking at Kaden with a one-word answer, "Good," before leaving.

His body felt hot all over and tingled where Logan's hand had held his wrist. His pulse beat through his veins faster, and he took a long drink of his ice-cold lemonade, trying to cool himself off internally. The afternoon went faster than he wanted, and he spent some time cleaning up the house, even going into Logan's room to clean up the clothes that lay all over the floor. He tried to keep up in there as much as possible, doing laundry every week to ensure that the man stayed in clean clothes. It amazed him how much of a slob Logan actually was. But he supposed it had to be expected since he spent so much time working the ranch and usually came home exhausted. He lovingly thumbed through the shirts in Logan's closet, breathing in deeply of the man's cologne that he never went without. It was a strong, spicy scent that Kaden couldn't seem to get enough of. The bed remained unmade, the quilt thrown aside in his haste to get to Kaden last night.

Kaden slowly made the bed, his cheeks flushing and his

breathing getting heavier as he thought of Logan lying in that big bed. He bit his lip when he felt his flesh stir, and he backed away, trying to get a hold on himself. There was nothing wrong with being attracted to the man, the voice in his heart shouted at him, but of course, his mind, the forever sensible one, screamed at him to stop being stupid. Passion meant pain. Passion meant being used and hurt. Struggling with himself internally, Kaden picked up the basket of laundry and made his way down the stairs. He started the first load and set the next one aside, ready for the washer.

To distract himself from his thoughts, he grabbed a book off the shelf in the living room and settled down into the easy chair near the couch to read for a while. It was a gripping novel about a vampire and a detective who misunderstood his intentions, believing him to be evil. It ended with the vampire and the detective becoming lovers, and the detective realizing that the vampire wasn't out to hurt people. That he only took what he needed to survive, leaving them alive.

The men spent dinner, the usual boisterous affair, bragging about what they intended to do that night and on their day off. Charlie had another date in town, which Kaden knew had to be with the lady from the grocery store. He heard some of the men talking about heading over to the honky-tonk to see if they could get lucky. Some of the men spoke of having a poker game, and one of them wanted to run out and get some beer and snacks. One of the men asked Logan what he intended to do that night and the next day, and Logan just gave them a smirk. They all started ribbing him, teasing him about getting laid and asking who the lucky lady was. Logan brushed their words off with a careless shrug. "Believe what you want, fellows. I don't intend to share my personal life with you."

"Who's it with? That sexy brunette from the beauty salon?" one man called, and another gave a shrill whistle of appreciation.

"She's one fine-lookin' lady. I wouldn't mind takin' a crack at that one myself."

Logan glared at the man who said that. "Don't even try it, Grainger. I'll kick your ass if you hurt her."

Kaden hid a smile behind his glass of tea at Logan's words and the fierceness behind them. It had taken two months, but Kaden had decided to stop hiding in the kitchen, and tonight, for the first time, he sat with everyone else, much to Logan's surprise and happiness. The men had been quiet at first, coughing nervously, before they'd started opening up in front of him. And now they sat there talking like he had always been one of the crew, which made him feel accepted, and of course, they immediately complimented him on his cooking, telling him he needed to come back next year. They had no idea that Logan intended to keep him there all year round no matter what it took. Before long, the men wandered off to do their own thing, telling the boss they'd see him Monday morning. Tension invaded Kaden, and he knew he couldn't stall much longer. He started to do the dishes. Logan helped him by bringing in the ones from the dining room, and then helping to dry them and put them away.

It wasn't but another hour before Logan and Kaden sat in the living room on the sofa. Kaden felt nervous as hell, and twisted his fingers together. "You don't have to talk if you don't want to," Logan said, his eyes not missing the anxiety or the nervous movements.

"No. I want to!" Kaden exclaimed, taking a deep breath before starting his story.

Yet Kaden still hesitated and stood abruptly to walk over to the fireplace, studying the photos atop the mantel. He smiled humorlessly, tracing the edge of one of the frames. "You know, when I first came here, I thought that you guys had the perfect life, the perfect family. That you had what I might have had if my parents hadn't died. Then I find out your life wasn't all that I thought it was."

His gaze remained trained on the photo, aware of Logan's on him. He couldn't bear to look Logan in the eyes just yet. Not until the story had been told in its entirety. "My father died before I was born in a car accident. My mom used to tell me about him all the time, and even though I had never met him, I idolized him. But as with all things, life went on, and my mother met another man and got married. His name was Gary, and he seemed like a cool guy, only what my mother didn't know was that the bastard turned out to be a pedophile."

He tensed when he heard Logan's indrawn breath. His lips twisted cruelly as he went on, "He would sneak into my room at night and... do things to me. I feared him, and what he threatened to do to me if I ever told my mother, so I stayed quiet. My mother died of cancer just after I had turned ten, leaving me with him. Once she had passed away, the last thing standing in his way was gone, and he could do whatever he wanted to me. "

Logan's anger started to simmer, rising to the surface as he watched Kaden speaking. Even though Kaden hadn't told him details in those sentences, he could only imagine the horrors that he had suffered. His hands clenched in the fabric of the sofa, and he tried to keep his emotions calm, not wanting to upset Kaden. He could see the boy's hands were shaking, and it seemed as though Kaden wasn't in the room with him anymore. He'd returned to where that bastard had hurt him.

Kaden's voice trembled as he continued telling Logan his past, "N-nothing could have prepared me for what happened in the next five years. He would force me to do things to him, force me to touch him. When I refused, or I fought back, he would hit me, cut me with knives or razor blades. Cigars were his favorite. He used those all over my body. He said he wanted to make me ugly to the world so they wouldn't try to take me away from him."

A shudder ran through Kaden, and tears welled up as he brought his hand to his cheek. "One night, he got so drunk that he beat me and raped me for what felt like the millionth time, but this time, he left a wound visible to the world." His fingers trailed over the scar, feeling the ragged edges.

"He'd always been so careful to keep the cuts, burns, and bruises where they would be hidden beneath my clothing, but this time, he had no idea what he was doing. His words to me that night ring in my head in my nightmares. 'Now no one will want you. You're mine.'" Kaden's voice held bitterness, and tears rolled down his cheeks, dripping onto his shirt. "He passed out, and I ran from the house, running down the street until I fainted from loss of blood. The next thing I knew, I woke up in the hospital to find my stepfather in the room with me."

Kaden stopped, his hands gripping the stone mantelpiece. He breathed deeply, trying to keep himself from hyperventilating. His breathing had already become shallow, and he felt dizzy from the overload of emotions. "He told them that I hadn't come home that night, and they assumed that someone had attacked me, a bully from my school, or someone had tried to mug me. In shock, I couldn't bring myself to dispute what they said. So he took me home, and the pattern repeated for another year before it came to a shatteringly abrupt halt when I was fifteen. I… Gary came home from the bar, reeking of alcohol again. I'd already fallen asleep by then, and he came into my r-room. I woke to find him on top of me, struggling to strip my clothes o-off."

"Stop," Logan demanded, standing up, wincing when he saw Kaden flinch. He moved to Kaden's side, gathering him close to his chest. "It's obvious that the bastard had problems, and—"

Kaden interrupted him, continuing with the events that had unfolded that night.

"Something inside me snapped. I felt as if I wasn't really in my body, as if someone else had control of me, and the next thing I knew, there were policemen and ambulances outside my home. Apparently one of the neighbors heard me screaming and called the police. I k-k-killed him, Logan." Kaden's hands fisted in Logan's shirt, his lips trembling with memories. The flashing lights from the police cruisers, the sirens, and the flash of cameras all played in his mind. "They found me stabbing him, over and over again. They had to force me to let go of the knife, and let them take me out. I was covered in blood from head to toe. His blood. My hands, my face, everything." He started to cry, great gasping cries.

Logan picked Kaden up as if he weighed nothing and brought him over to the sofa, sitting down with Kaden's legs stretched across his lap and part of the couch. He cradled Kaden's head against his chest and held him tightly. He rubbed Kaden's back soothingly, trying to get him to settle down, to stop crying. "It's all right, Kaden. That son of a bitch deserved it and a hell of a lot more. You did it in self-defense, and no one can blame you for it." His breath ruffled the dark strands of hair on top of Kaden's head, and he waited for Kaden to calm, his body shivering every once in a while.

Kaden's voice had dropped to a mere whisper as he finished, his throat raw from the crying jag. "They placed me in an institution for two years. They said that it took them months to get me to respond to anything, and that I just sat there and stared at my hands. It took two full years of visits to a psychiatrist, and medicines to 'rehabilitate' me. Fear of large men has kept me moving from job to job. I couldn't keep a single job for more than a week or two, if lucky. Every night, I see his face, and I see what I did to him. I see the police looking at me with pity in their eyes and the other kids I met in that hospital."

Logan slid his hand beneath Kaden's chin, forcing his head up to meet his gaze. "You are a beautiful and strong person,

Kaden. You didn't deserve what that sick bastard did to you, but you have me and Shea now, and we'll take care of you. And if you think that I'm going to let you go just because of the horrible things you had to endure as a child, you had better stop thinking that, because I never intend to let you go, Kaden. I wish I could change it, and take away everything bad that ever happened to you. I would trade anything I have for that ability."

The violet eyes shimmered with emotions, warring between disbelief and hope. Logan wasn't disgusted by him, and he still wanted him to stay. He snuggled closer to Logan, a tired smile playing at the corners of his mouth. "I was so scared that you would think me disgusting or like I had asked for it to happen."

"No one asks to be a victim, Kaden. I'm glad you told me, and I hope that in time you'll be able to trust me enough to give yourself to me." Logan leaned his head back against the couch, keeping a tight hold on the teenager in his lap.

They sat there, embracing one another, for the longest time. When Kaden pulled away and went to stand, Logan stopped him by gripping his wrist lightly. "Will you let me hold you tonight?" the cowboy asked him quietly. His green eyes were serious and seemed to look straight inside Kaden's heart.

Kaden nodded, and they made sure they'd locked the doors and the lights were out before making their way upstairs to Logan's room. Once inside the bedroom, Logan smiled reassuringly at him and went to change into a pair of sweatpants and a T-shirt. Kaden kicked off his sneakers and his jeans, leaving only boxers and his T-shirt, before slipping between the covers. He lay there, tense, and staring at the ceiling when Logan came back out. Logan flipped the light switch off and moved over to the other side of the bed, slipping in beside Kaden. Logan pulled him carefully, tenderly into his side, pressing a small kiss to Kaden's temple. "Good night, my little one."

"Good night, Logan," Kaden breathed, closing his eyes and trying to relax. He still suffered from insomnia, and he listened to Logan's breathing even out as he fell asleep. He started in surprise when the big man subconsciously pulled him closer, the arms surrounding him and dragging him against the broad chest.

Eventually, Kaden drifted off to sleep, a tranquil, dreamless sleep. The sense of someone looking at him woke him from that peaceful rest, and his eyes slowly blinked open to find green eyes watching him sleep. He flushed at the intense scrutiny, and ducked his head beneath Logan's chin, enjoying the deep chuckle that rumbled from the strong chest. "Good morning. Did you sleep well?" Logan's honeyed voice sounded raspy with sleep, drifting over his senses and making him feel safe.

He nodded and almost sighed with absolute pleasure when he felt one of Logan's strong hands begin to stroke his back, rubbing gently and massaging him. "Shea mentioned you wanted to have me set up that punching bag I talked about, and for me to show you some of the judo moves. Would you like to start that today?"

"Okay," Kaden murmured, breathing in the scent of Logan's skin. He could feel the hard body pressing against him so intimately from chest to thighs to legs. It was the most erotically simple moment he'd ever experienced. He still could not believe that Logan hadn't been disgusted with him after finding out that he'd murdered his own stepfather. The courts had deemed it temporary insanity after researching with neighbors and teachers, finding out that the stepfather had in fact been sexually and physically abusing him. "Logan?"

"Hmm?"

"Would you... ah... would you... kiss me?" His cheeks burned brightly with embarrassment, and he felt Logan's body vibrate with the deep laugh that issued from his lungs.

Logan gently rolled him onto his back, leaning over him

slightly, without putting his entire body on top of him. His eyes twinkled with amusement as he gazed down at Kaden's adorable flushed face. He reached up one hand to slide his thumb over the soft skin of Kaden's cheek before slowly lowering his head, his eyes becoming half-slits in anticipation and desire. He brushed his own lips across Kaden's, pulling back before diving forward again, teasing both himself and Kaden. He tasted, he savored, and then drank greedily of the pale pink lips beneath his. Logan darted his tongue out to lick lightly at the full bottom lip, sucking it between his lips and tugging on it with each soft pull of his mouth. Lust blazed through him when he heard Kaden's moan, and the boy's hands came up to tangle in his sandy hair.

Heat infused Logan's body, each beat of his pulse sending even more liquid fire racing through him, and he wanted nothing more than to ravish Kaden's sweet little body underneath him, but he reluctantly pulled away, resisting Kaden's attempts to pull him in for more. He slid his index finger over the length of Kaden's nose. "Sorry, baby, but if we keep at it like that I'm... not going to be able to hold back."

It took a second for Logan's words to sink in, and when they did Kaden's eyes widened in a flash of fear and shock. "I'm sorry," he whispered, turning his head aside.

Logan turned his head back toward him, gazing down into the saddened violet eyes. "Don't be sorry, Kaden. Never be sorry. I'll survive. And I don't want to do anything that will scare you or hurt you. So we're taking this one little step at a time. You taste so good that my body craves yours like a dying man craves water, but I can control myself." He smiled to show Kaden that he wasn't upset or mad. "Time to get up, little one. We've got some work to do, and we're already burning daylight hours here."

With that, Logan lifted himself from the bed, tugging Kaden behind him. He turned Kaden to face the bedroom door and with a gentle push, said, "Go. Get dressed. I'll see you downstairs for breakfast. I'm making, so don't touch anything." He pressed a small kiss to the back of Kaden's neck before turning to stride into his own bathroom, closing the door until there was only a gap.

Kaden smiled happily and raced out of the room. Shea stepped out of the bathroom as Kaden walked past. She grinned from ear to ear when she saw him leaving Logan's room in nothing but a T-shirt and boxers. "Good morning, Kaden," she called out cheerfully as she sailed into her bedroom, shutting the door behind her.

He shook his head at her enthusiasm at her brother being with another man, and darted down the stairs, heading to his room. Dressed and in the kitchen, Kaden had started making coffee, by the time Logan came downstairs. Warm arms enclosed him tightly, and then Logan's voice brushed over his ear. "I thought I told you not to touch anything."

"But it's just coffee! And I can't survive without at least one cup!" Kaden exclaimed, not able to see the teasing look in Logan's eyes.

"I was only teasing, baby." Logan nipped gently at the side of Kaden's neck, grinning like an idiot when he felt the shudder of pleasure go through Kaden, before pulling back to go start breakfast. Logan felt so happy that he literally wanted to shout his joy to the world, but he restrained himself, not wanting to seem like he'd gone insane. He felt Kaden watching him, and it made him feel good to know that he'd made the younger man happy. Kaden had certainly smiled more in the last few days than he had in the entire two months he'd been on the ranch.

CHAPTER 12

BREAKFAST turned out to be just the two of them, Shea apparently having decided to sleep in, and Kaden helped Logan with the dishes when they were finished eating, leaving a plate for Shea in the microwave, and a note on the stove telling her where it was. Logan led him out to the barn to get the supplies he needed. He had an old punching bag in the hayloft from when he'd practiced his own moves. He motioned for Kaden to go up the ladder first, grinned at the sight of the tantalizing rear end that swished in front of his eyes as Kaden slowly climbed into the loft. He enjoyed the scenery the entire way up. He wanted nothing more than to push Kaden down into the hay and kiss him senseless again, but controlled himself because not only would he have to go take another cold shower like this morning, he might frighten Kaden.

With the horses in the barn, Logan set the punching bag up outside, to keep from spooking them when he hit the bag. Logan watched the eagerness in Kaden's expression, and the way he seemed so ready to take his pain out on the inanimate object instead of himself. It made his heart swell inside his chest to know that the teenager had healed so much since he'd come to the ranch. He would have to make sure to call his cousin and thank him for sending the kid to him. They spent the rest of the afternoon with

Logan directing him on how to kick and punch the bag, and sweat poured off of Kaden by then, but he had a big, happy smile on his face.

Kaden brushed his hair back from his face with the back of his hand and looked to Logan, "Thank you."

"For what?" Logan asked, leaning on the fence nearby, just enjoying watching Kaden move.

"For helping me. For being there for me. It's been... a long time since someone cared about me." Kaden cast his eyes to the side, uncomfortable.

"Like I said, we are your family now. And we care for our own. If you ever need anything, just ask, Kaden. I'm serious."

Nodding, Kaden looked back up at Logan, and then looked over at Mantacor. The horse stood near the fence, watching him and Logan warily, waiting to see if the man was going to do anything to him. Kaden looked around the ranch and back at Logan, awed that he'd gone from having nothing to having so much in such a short time. It made him fear losing it. But he held it to his heart, enjoying the comfort and happiness while it lasted. His experiences had always shown him it never lasted.

Another two weeks came and went, bringing roundup closer to an end. Kaden spent a good portion of his time when he wasn't cooking using the punching bag that Logan had set up for him. It had become something of a ritual, and it made him feel good. Logan and Kaden spent most of their free time together whenever they weren't busy with ranch work. Kaden had started to smile more and gained a bit more self-confidence in who he was and where he stood with Logan, though he had started to notice that Logan only touched him when they were alone. He almost went out of his way not to be too comfortable with him when Shea or the hands were around. The thought that Logan might be embarrassed of their relationship bothered him, but he tried to keep it to himself, not wanting to upset Logan. Maybe the cowboy wasn't ready to admit to his friends that he was involved with another man. Kaden tried to concentrate on just enjoying their time together.

But he should have known better than to underestimate Logan. "What's wrong?" Logan asked quietly one night while they were sitting in the living room watching a movie together.

Kaden looked up in surprise. "What?"

"Something's wrong. I can see it in the look on your face sometimes, and it's been bothering you for a while now. Tell me what's wrong." Logan stopped the movie and turned his body toward Kaden, taking his slender hand in his larger one, stroking his thumb over Kaden's wrist, where the scars lay. The wristband had long since been removed.

His mind warring over whether or not he should say anything, Kaden sat there in an extended silence. Would Logan get angry at his stupid worries? Taking a deep breath and averting his eyes away from Logan, he tried to pull his hand away. But Logan held on firmly, and Kaden stuttered, "I… um… it's just something stupid."

"Nothing is stupid if it worries you. You can tell me anything, no matter how small or unimportant you may think it is. I want you to know that."

"Well… I… just wondered if… maybe you were… um… ashamed to admit… to everyone that you're… involved with me." Kaden held his breath, his eyes still trained on a small spot on the carpet. He almost gasped when he felt a strong and warm hand slide beneath his chin, gently turning his head so that his gaze met Logan's. Hurt shone clearly from Logan's eyes, and Kaden let out the breath in a sigh of surprise.

Logan looked over the pale features of Kaden's face, tracing the eyebrows, lush lips, and the scar with his gaze. Uncertainty shimmered in the bright violet depths, and he couldn't deny he'd been hurt to learn Kaden would believe that. He supposed he could understand since he never really touched Kaden affectionately whenever the men were around, but it was more for the boy's sake than anything else. "I would never be ashamed to admit that to anyone, Kaden. It pains me to hear you say that or that you've been thinking it for so long now without talking to me about it. I have only been thinking of you when it comes to the men and even Shea. I don't want you to feel pressured or uncomfortable. I only want to further our intimacy when you feel you're ready."

Kaden watched as Logan's lips twisted wryly as he continued speaking. "My body is feeling the strain, but no matter what, it's up to you when we take it to the next level. Even if we never do, I will never ever pressure you for anything you don't think you're ready for."

Kaden realized what Logan meant, and shame overcame him. He hung his head, looking down at where Logan's hand still grasped his. "I'm sorry," he mumbled.

"Don't be. I told you, no matter what, I want you to talk to me. Promise me you'll do that?" The cowboy's voice had moved closer to his ear, and Kaden jerked slightly, turning his head to find his mouth no more than an inch away from Logan's.

"I... I promise." Kaden's breath whispered across Logan's lips, and struck with the urge to kiss the gentle cowboy, he leaned closer, aligning his lips with Logan's.

He felt Logan's immediate response in the firming of his lips, and their tongues danced over each other, pressing close before darting away to explore each other's mouths. Kaden almost groaned when he felt Logan's warm hand cup the back of his neck, pulling him deeper into the heated kiss. He pushed further into Logan, reaching a hand out to tentatively caress the broad, muscular chest. He lightly trailed his fingers over the man's collar bone, traveling lower to run over the hard pecs, and he felt Logan shudder when his palm accidentally brushed over one of his hard nipples. Teasingly, he did it again, enjoying the reaction it elicited from Logan.

Logan broke the kiss, panting with desire, his cock hard as stone, and he grabbed Kaden's hand. "No more," he pleaded, closing his eyes and leaning his head back against the couch cushion.

Kaden moved to straddle Logan's legs, causing Logan's eyes to fly open in astonishment. "What are you doing, Kaden?" His voice came out rough with trying to rein in his lust, not wanting to scare Kaden with the depth of his passion for the boy.

Smiling, Kaden leaned forward, kissing Logan again, and he brought his hands down to continue with his previous actions. Logan clenched his hands on the couch beside his thighs, digging his nails into his palms to keep from grabbing the teenager and slinging him beneath him to bury his aching length deep inside him. He sucked in a deep breath when the back of Kaden's slim fingers brushed over the bulge in his jeans. He grabbed Kaden's hands, holding them away from him. Through gritted teeth, he said, "Stop. You don't know what you're doing to me."

"I do know," the dark-haired teenager panted, his eyes glittering like amethysts with his own passion. "I... may not be ready for everything... but I want to do something for you, Logan. Please let me."

Logan groaned in capitulation, releasing Kaden's hands and gripping the slender thighs straddling his waist as Kaden started to kiss his neck, the small pink tongue flicking out to lave the saltiness from his skin. He almost let out a cry of relief when Kaden released his stiff prick from his jeans, but he couldn't stifle the one he let out when those pale fingers wrapped around his flesh. The inexperienced fingers fumbled over his silken shaft before tightening and beginning to tug. He felt Kaden's teeth nip at his throat before soothing it, his tongue dancing over his sensitive skin.

Kaden felt a wetness slide down Logan's hard length, causing his palm to slicken against the cowboy's cock. He continued to caress him, rocking his own hips forward. He felt Logan's hands slide up his thighs to grip his ass, the long, thick fingers pressing into his flesh. A red heat flashed through him, and his breathing grew heavy. Sweat gathered on both of their bodies, glistening in the light from the lamp on the side table and from the TV screen, where the movie sat frozen in time. Kaden could feel Logan shuddering, and the muscles in his body tensing. His hand moved faster, tightening a little more, when he realized the blond approached his release.

Grunting, Logan arched from the couch, still gripping Kaden's body in a punishing embrace, his come spilling across his and Kaden's shirts, and the slim fingers still pleasuring him. Finally, he moved his hand to still Kaden's, his cock overly sensitive after the hard orgasm. Kaden kept his face buried in the side of Logan's neck, a flush of lust covering his cheeks. "Thank you," he heard Logan breathe.

Neither of them moved for a long moment until Kaden felt Logan's hands moving up to massage his back, slipping beneath his T-shirt. His eyes widened and he jerked away, almost falling off Logan's lap and into the coffee table in his haste to get away. "Kaden?" Logan queried in astonishment.

"I... I'm sorry. I...." Kaden wrapped his arms around his waist, hugging himself as tight as he could. He didn't want Logan to see his body. Such a beautiful man should not have to lay his eyes on such a monster.

Logan fixed his clothes before standing up to move over to the teen's side. He placed a soothing hand on Kaden's shoulder. "Did I move too fast?"

Kaden gave a furious shake of his head. "No," he replied

tensely, knowing that his answer wouldn't appease Logan and that he would push him for a specific reason.

"Then why did you jump off of me like you were on fire?" the cowboy teased lightly.

"Be… because my body is disgusting."

Before another word could be uttered, Kaden found himself swept up in Logan's arms and brought back to the couch. Logan settled Kaden on his lap and started to rain little kisses all over Kaden's face. "You could never be disgusting. You're beautiful."

"But—" Kaden didn't finish what he'd been about to say when Logan's lips descended on his, and then he felt Logan's big hand sliding beneath the front of his T-shirt. He gave a mew of distress, trying to stop Logan.

"Relax, little one. I want to touch you. Like you touched me." That honeyed voice dropped a curtain of desire over Kaden's senses, and he relented, shame flooding his features when Logan pushed the hem of his shirt up, baring his stomach. He sucked in a sharp breath when he felt, for the first time, Logan's hot skin against the smooth flesh of his belly.

Logan stifled his rage when he saw the scars that covered Kaden's stomach, not wanting to cause Kaden to believe for a split second his emotions were anything close to disgust. For Logan, it couldn't be further from the truth. His body begged him to take Kaden where they sat, demanding to feel the younger man's body surrounding him. He slowly moved his hand, the shirt sliding up in the process, further up, baring more of the teen's childhood torment. A thrill raced through him when he heard Kaden let out a moan at the sweep of his palm over the dark-haired man's hard nipples. "You like that?" he whispered into Kaden's ear, doing it again and feeling a shiver run through the teen's body.

Kaden nodded, still feeling embarrassed. Logan's hand felt wonderfully sinful on his skin, and when it cupped his cock through his pants, a gasp tripped from his lips. He felt the fingers moving and fondling him slowly, caressing him, driving him insane with pleasure. He let out a sound of protest when Logan took his hand away. "Shh. I'm just going to take away the barriers." Logan sounded amused, and Kaden bit his lip at his wanton behavior.

The button came out easily, and the zipper was loud enough to match the breath panting from Kaden's lungs. He felt the tugs at his clothing by Logan's hands, moving them down until his stiff cock came free from its confines. "Beautiful," he heard Logan murmur, and then one finger trailed along the length of the shaft.

Electricity darted over his body, sending sensations tingling down his spine. Kaden let out a hoarse cry when Logan's palm fisted his aching cock, slowly, tantalizingly beginning to tug. Each tug pulled at something in Kaden's stomach, twisting him higher and tighter. Heat invaded his groin, and his toes curled inside his socks. Stars began to dazzle him behind his eyelids, which had slid closed after the first tug.

Logan couldn't look away from Kaden's flushed face, the pale lips parted with his panting breaths, a light sheen of sweat dampening the skin, causing his dark hair to stick to his face. He had never seen anything so wonderful, so exquisitely stunning. The soft, slick skin beneath his palm pulsed as Kaden stepped closer and closer to that edge, the moment you let go of the world and everything faded but the wonder of flying. A shudder of Kaden's body was his only warning, and his eyes flickered to where their bodies were connected, watching as the teen fell off the precipice, a cry of completion filling the room. White seed spilled across his hand, his shirt, and Kaden's jeans, adding to the mess they'd already made.

CHAPTER 13

KADEN lay there, dazed and astounded at how good it all had felt. Nothing he'd experienced had ever prepared him for the satiation and pleasure inundating his body. Shyness swamped him, and he kept his eyes closed. "Are you all right?" Logan asked softly.

"Uh huh." He had no other words. They'd been stolen by the breathtaking beauty of his first mutual orgasm.

"Were you scared? Did it feel good?"

He could hear uncertainty in Logan's voice, and finally found the courage to open his eyes. He grinned up at Logan, his gaze twinkling with merriment. "No, I wasn't scared. And hell yes, it felt good."

Logan released a sigh of relief, nuzzling Kaden's throat for a moment before pulling back to grimace at the mess they had made. "I think we should get cleaned up. We got a little dirty."

Kaden laughed and went to stand, but Logan scooped him up before he could move off him completely. "Together," Logan said, his tone brooking no argument.

Unease flittered over Kaden, but he knew he had to show Logan he trusted him, so he nodded. Logan gave him a wide, unabashed grin and juggled Kaden in his arms enough to lean over and turn off the TV and the light. He strode toward the stairs with purpose, heading up to his bathroom for privacy. Shea wouldn't be home for another hour at least, but he didn't want to take any chances at Kaden being embarrassed or ashamed. He set Kaden on his feet gently, reaching in to turn on the water and let it heat up before stripping his clothes off.

His eyes glued to the hard, chiseled body being revealed to him, Kaden stood there, his arms crossed over his belly. Logan turned and spotted him fully dressed, stalking slowly toward him. "You're still wearing clothes," he pointed out, his voice slightly accusing.

Kaden's hands shook, and he still hesitated to remove his shirt. But Logan took that choice from him when he stopped in front of him and grasped the hem of Kaden's shirt. "Lift your arms."

He complied reluctantly, and Logan slid the shirt over his head. His pale skin was littered with scars, varying in size and shape, from his shoulders to his chest and lower still to his belly. His arms came down to cover his chest as much as possible, but Logan gently gripped his wrists, pulling them away from his body. He felt the cowboy's lips settle against one of the scars. "Never hide yourself from me, Kaden. You're beautiful. And even if I have to kiss every single mark on your body to make you believe that, I will do it until the day we die."

Logan's hands dropped to his jeans, sliding them down his legs and encouraging him to step out of them. He now stood naked in front of Logan, who in turn led him into the shower and beneath the spray. Kaden had never felt as cherished as he did during the next twenty minutes. Logan soaped up his body, carefully washing each and every inch, from his neck down to his feet, squatting down to wash them. When Logan massaged his scalp with shampoo, Kaden couldn't stifle a small sigh of pleasure. It felt good, and he could feel the man's body leaning against his, sending a deliciously sinful shiver down his spine. But Logan didn't try to pursue any more physical contact, just finished washing him up before quickly taking care of his own body.

He wrapped Kaden up in a big fluffy towel, drying him gently and carefully, littering his shoulders and the back of his neck with butterfly kisses. When he'd finished, he slapped Kaden lightly on the butt and said, "Go, get in bed. I'll be there in a moment. I just have to use the bathroom."

Kaden gave him an indignant look over the ass slap and stuck out his tongue before darting out into the bedroom and climbing beneath the sheets. He snuggled down and closed his eyes, exhausted from the day's events. It didn't take long before he slipped into a deep sleep. He never even felt Logan sliding in beside him, or the strong arms that wrapped around him, dragging him back into the warm, hard body.

Sunlight streaming in the window the next morning woke Kaden, and he blinked, confused for a moment about where he was. A warm body pressed against his back, and he remembered the events of the previous evening. The heated moments with Logan on the couch, the wonderfully erotic shower, and sliding beneath the covers of Logan's bed, naked, all came back to him. He lay there for a moment, just enjoying the safe, warm feeling. Today he wanted to show Logan exactly what he'd accomplished with Mantacor. Excitement and pride wound through him. He couldn't wait to see Logan's expression when he saw Kaden astride the white stallion. Secretly, with Shea's help so that Logan wouldn't be angry with him, he had been working with Mantacor on trusting him more, accepting a saddle, and letting him ride him. Of course, he'd fallen off a few times due to Mantacor's fear of letting someone close to him, but eventually, after a few days of working with the animal, he'd managed to mount the horse and ride him around the corral. Kaden didn't trust the stallion enough yet to take him out of the corral, but at least he'd made progress. It would only be a matter of time before he could actually take Mantacor for a true run.

Kaden shifted to his side to face Logan when he heard the cowboy waking up. Propping his head up on one hand, Kaden watched as Logan slowly came to consciousness, the brow furrowing against the light splashed across his face, his eyes squinting shut a little tighter, and then the lips parting on a sigh as his eyelids slid open. Logan blinked a few times to clear his vision, his lips quirking up in a sleepy smile at Kaden. He reached out and lightly caressed Kaden's cheek. "Good morning, little one."

"Morning, Logan. Get up. I have something I want to show you after breakfast," Kaden said excitedly, unaware of the picture he presented with his hair disheveled, his cheeks flushed, and his eyes sparkling with his eagerness.

Just as Kaden went to leap from the bed, Logan gripped his wrist, pulling him beneath him before Kaden could even react. Kaden blinked owlishly up at Logan in surprise at suddenly being underneath the cowboy. Logan felt relief at the obvious lack of fear in the violet eyes. "You're supposed to give me a kiss good morning," he pointed out with a devilish grin.

The corners of Kaden's lips curved upward, and he wrinkled his nose at Logan. "We both have morning breath. At least let me brush my teeth first."

"No." Logan lowered his head, feathering his lips over Kaden's before deepening the kiss and thrusting his tongue into the depths of the boy's mouth.

A soft moan issued from Kaden's throat, and he brought his arms up around Logan's neck, threading his fingers in the sandy blond hair. Their skin slid against each other, the friction causing both of them to gasp simultaneously. Kaden felt Logan's cock stabbing his thigh, and panic rushed in. He nervously pulled away from Logan, closing his eyes and turning his head away. The cowboy relented, rolling to his back and flinging an arm over his face. "I'm sorry, Kaden. I didn't mean to frighten you."

"It's all right. I'm the one who should be apologizing. I know that it can't be easy for you to have to deal with my stupid—" Logan's hand came over his mouth, muffling whatever he would have said.

A glint of anger flickered in the intense green eyes as Logan reprimanded him fiercely. "Don't ever apologize for being afraid. Not after everything you've gone through. I do not want to ever hear you say those words again."

Kaden nodded weakly, his eyes wide and his lips quivering as Logan lifted his hand away. "Go. Go get dressed, and you can show me this surprise after we eat," Logan said wearily, brushing the backs of his index and middle finger down Kaden's arm.

Logan watched as the teen scrambled from the bed, hurriedly putting on his jeans and grabbing the rest of his clothes before darting out of the bedroom. He flopped back onto the bed and cursed himself, calling himself every name he could think of for being such an idiot. But the boy had been so tempting that he hadn't been able to resist. It would take time to gain Kaden's trust, and be able to make love with him. He accepted that, but his body wanted to ignore what his mind told it. Sighing with resignation, he headed into the bathroom to take the thousandth cold shower since the younger man's arrival.

Kaden hummed happily as he began to fix breakfast, a smile hovering on his lips no matter how much he tried to school his expression. Nothing could make him sad right now. He stared out the window above the sink, catching sight of Mantacor dancing around in his corral, tossing his long mane and flicking his tail with happiness in the early morning sunshine. "Someone sounds happy this morning!" he heard Shea chirp behind him, and Kaden turned to smile at her.

144

"Good morning, Shea. I'm going to show Logan this morning, so you have to keep him inside while I get everything ready," he informed her as he slid eggs and bacon onto three plates before adding two slices of toast each.

"That's great, Kaden!" Shea walked over to grab the glasses for orange juice out of the cabinet, setting them on the table before grabbing the jug from the fridge.

Kaden poured himself and Logan a cup of coffee while she set out the silverware on the small kitchen table. Logan stepped into the kitchen just as the two of them were sitting down to eat. He dropped a tired kiss on top of Shea's head and slid into the chair next to Kaden. "So what's this surprise?" he asked as he started to eat.

He saw the looks that passed between Kaden and Shea, secretive looks. "You'll have to wait, big brother." Shea winked at him and stuffed a bite of toast in her mouth.

Logan could see the pride and satisfaction in Kaden over his surprise, and warmth settled low in his belly as he watched the excitement in Kaden. The boy could barely sit still, and as soon as he was done eating, he stood up, washing his own plate and fork. "I'm going to go get everything ready," he said, flitting out the door before Logan could say anything.

He looked over at his sister in question, but she just smiled smugly and finished up her breakfast. "Don't move from that chair until I tell you to," she said, washing her dishes and grabbing his when he finished. She watched out the window while she washed the dishes, and Logan couldn't figure it out for the life of him. "Okay, bro. Time to go." She grabbed his hand and tugged him from the chair. "Close your eyes!"

He rolled his eyes but obeyed, falling sedately behind Shea. She led him down the porch steps and across the hard, packed dirt. "Open your eyes," she cried, and he opened them to find Kaden sitting astride Mantacor. His eyes widened, and his heart began to pound.

"What in the hell do you think you're doing?" he shouted, startling Mantacor slightly.

Kaden's wide smile of accomplishment faded, and he stared with hurt at Logan. "I… I'm sorry. I thought you'd be happy. I didn't do it alone. Shea helped me the entire time."

Logan swung his head to glare at his sister. "What the hell were you thinking, Shea? He could have been seriously hurt! That horse is dangerous."

Shea's hands came up to her hips, the defiant stance matching the pissed off look on her face. "You really are an idiot, Logan. In case you haven't noticed, that horse adores him. Mantacor would never hurt Kaden on purpose. He's as docile with Kaden as Brandy is with me! Now look what you've done! Kaden, get back on the horse."

The entire time that the siblings had been arguing, Kaden's heart had fallen into his stomach, and he slowly dismounted, undoing the straps on the saddle. Mantacor gave him a look of questioning but he just smiled weakly. He patted the horse's neck lightly. "It's okay, boy. I'll take you for a ride another day."

Logan felt like an asshole at the disheartened expression on Kaden's face.

"I'm sorry, Kaden. Please show me what you've accomplished." Not only had he frightened the boy that morning, he'd screwed up yet again. But seeing him on that horse's back had almost made his heart stop. If something happened to Kaden, he didn't know what he would do.

Kaden looked at him, studying him for a moment. "It's all right. I'll just show you another day."

"No. Please. I want to see it now." Logan tried to encourage him with a smile, kicking his own ass mentally. The boy had been so happy and proud of being able to ride the horse, and he'd reacted like such a jerk. Damn, it seemed that he was constantly screwing up when it came to Kaden.

The teen hesitated for another second before starting to redo the straps, making sure they were tight before swinging up into the saddle. Kaden began to smile again, slowly at first, as he put Mantacor through the paces that Shea had shown him. He felt such peace being astride the sweet animal. No one understood that the horse just needed someone to understand him. Like Logan had with him. Mantacor tossed his head as if to say, "Look at me," and let out a neigh of pleasure, trotting around the corral with Kaden encouraging him. "Good boy, Mantacor. You're just a big softy, aren't you, boy," he said, smiling broadly at Shea and Logan.

Logan began to ease his grip on the fence the longer Kaden rode the horse. It appeared as though the stallion really did trust Kaden, and believed that Kaden wouldn't hurt him. It seemed that both of them had been healing slowly these last several weeks, together, with different catalysts. Real joy radiated brightly from Kaden's entire being, and Logan leaned against the fence to enjoy the sight.

After showing Logan all the things that Mantacor had learned, Kaden dismounted in the center of the ring and went to remove the saddle, but Mantacor darted away, stopping a few feet from him. Kaden frowned, approaching the horse once more, and as he reached out to grip the saddle again, Mantacor pranced another ten feet. Suddenly it dawned on Kaden why the stallion kept running from him. He was playing, teasing Kaden. He grinned. "So that's how it is, huh, boy? Well, let's see who can beat who, then." With that, he began to chase the horse, almost playing a form of tag with the animal.

Shea and Logan were laughing and calling encouragement to

Kaden, who in turn was laughing so hard it made it hard to keep up with the stallion, until finally, Mantacor seemed to tire of the game and let Kaden catch him. The teen removed the saddle and brushed the white horse down, patting his hindquarters before carrying the saddle into the barn. Shea headed back into the house, and Logan followed Kaden. He watched, arms folded, propped up against the barn door while the boy put away the saddle and reins. When Kaden came back out of the tack room, Logan praised him. "Well done, Kaden. You've managed to accomplish with that horse in just a few weeks what I've been trying to for over a year."

Kaden gave him a cheeky grin and teased, "Well, I just happen to have that magic touch, unlike an old guy like you."

Logan raised an eyebrow at his words. "An old guy like me, huh?" The cowboy pushed away from the door, slowly stalking Kaden, who started to back away, still grinning. Kaden found he had nowhere to go but up, so he grabbed hold of the ladder, and hoisting himself up, moved agilely up the rungs. Logan followed, intent on extracting revenge for the teen's insult. Kaden looked around frantically for a place to hide in the hay loft, and headed to the open overhead doors.

"You've got nowhere to go, Kaden," Logan taunted from the other side of the hay loft, a smug smile curving his lips.

Kaden waited for an opportunity to dart around Logan and go back down the ladder, taking the chance when he saw an opening, only to be stopped when an arm of steel came around his waist, tackling him down into the loose hay. Logan chuckled as he began to tickle Kaden, causing laughter to erupt from the dark-haired young man. He ran his fingers along the thin sides, brushing over the boy's ribs. Kaden tried to grab at Logan's hands to stop him. But the cowboy had more strength than he did, and he just rolled around, trying to dislodge his hands. "O-okay! I... gi-give," he cried out, fighting to breathe, his chest heaving from lack of oxygen.

Taking pity on him, Logan stopped, grinning down at Kaden, his hands still on the boy's sides. There were several strands of straw stuck to Kaden's head, and he slowly began to pick them off, tossing them aside. Light from the open door cast over Kaden's features, and his grin faded as he looked down into those violet eyes, the ones he loved so much, the ones he never wanted to see sad again. "I love you, Kaden," he whispered, bringing his lips down to meet Kaden's, brushing over them in a soft caress.

Shock wound its way through Kaden at Logan's words, and tears stung his eyes at the gentle giant's sweet confession. He brought his arms up, winding them around Logan's shoulders and deepened the kiss. They lay there, slowly kissing, without lust or passion, just simple, loving kisses.

Even though Kaden didn't say the words back, Logan felt in his heart that the boy cared for him in the same way he cared for the boy. It would just take time for him to voice his feelings.

Another turning point in their relationship came that night, much to Logan's surprise and absolute delight. After dinner, Shea left to go on another date with Ty, telling them not to wait up for her, to which Logan growled that she had better be joking. She'd laughed that tinkling laugh she gave sometimes before winking and racing out of the house before he could stop her.

CHAPTER 14

HAPPY that he and Logan had the house to themselves, Kaden tried to ignore the churning in his stomach. Something had changed inside him that morning. When Logan had uttered those words to him in the hayloft, the final chip of ice on his heart had given way, melting away to nothing. He knew that he'd fallen in love with the big cowboy, a head over heels, fireworks-exploding-in-the-air kind of love. The realization left him with the desire to be closer to him, to explore another side of their relationship in the physical sense. His fear hadn't just disappeared, and his hands shook as he washed the dishes from their dinner. Could he go through with it? It wouldn't be fair to Logan if he started and had to stop in the middle. Determination to show Logan that he held complete trust in him stiffened Kaden's spine, and he refused to allow his past to keep them from being together. He would just remind himself that Logan loved him, and would never hurt him, abuse him, or touch him with the intention of causing pain.

Logan could sense Kaden's nervousness and wondered if his confession that morning had upset him. It caused him to doubt his certainty that Kaden felt the same, and as always, he couldn't let Kaden brood over whatever had upset him, so Logan asked, "Is something wrong?"

"Hmm?" Kaden looked up from the dish he was drying only

to find Logan's eyes studying him intently. "N... no. Nothing's wrong. Why would you think that?"

"You seem awfully jumpy if nothing's wrong," Logan commented.

Logan reminded Kaden of a detective. He had a way of seeing things most people wouldn't. Or maybe he wore his emotions on his face like a coat on his body. Kaden had never been good at hiding his feelings. So he sighed and said, "Let me finish these, and then I'll show you what's wrong."

Logan's brow furrowed at the boy's choice of words, but he shrugged and stood up to help him finish the dishes. Once they'd been put away, Logan took Kaden by the hand and led him into the living room. "Now, tell me what's wrong."

Kaden didn't know quite how to put it, but he supposed he should just come out with it. Taking a deep breath, he looked Logan in the eyes and said, "I want you to make love to me."

"No," Logan refused stiffly, standing up to move restlessly around the room.

"B-but why? Don't you... want me?" Kaden asked hoarsely, fingering the hem of his T-shirt, his heart pounding hard and fast. He didn't understand the cowboy's denial of his request. Did Logan really mean everything he'd said? Or did Logan say those things about his body being beautiful just to give him confidence?

"Kaden, I want you more than anything else in this world, but I won't let you force yourself into something that you aren't ready for," Logan said heatedly, fiercely. His green eyes flashed, and his lips were turning white around the edges with how tightly he pulled them in.

"How do you know I'm not ready?" Kaden demanded, standing up straighter and glaring at Logan. "Why do you get to decide that? It's my body and my choice. I...." He softened his words, looking down at his shoes. "I want you, Logan. Truly, sincerely want you. Please." His voice had dipped to a mere breath of a whisper, and he blinked furiously, twisting his fingers in the hem of his shirt further.

Logan warred with his inner mind. He wanted to accept Kaden at his word so badly that it hurt, but how could the younger man truly know what he wanted? Sighing, he moved closer to Kaden, taking him gently into his arms and cradling him close to his chest. He rested his chin on top of the kid's head lightly. "Are you sure? Absolutely sure?"

"Yes."

He pulled back to gaze down at Kaden, a stern expression dominating his face. "If you feel afraid or uncomfortable, you are to tell me, immediately. Do you hear me?"

Nodding, Kaden beamed up at Logan, the grin beginning to fade as the emerald eyes darkened with passion. He licked his lips, wetting them and drawing those jewels to stare at his mouth. A squeak emerged from Kaden's throat when Logan suddenly swept him up in his arms and started up the stairs to his bedroom. Logan slowly set Kaden on his feet, brushing a lock of dark hair back from his face before lowering his lips to cover Kaden's. Kaden reached up to wrap his arms around Logan's neck, his fingers twining in the sandy blond hair as they kissed.

Heat started building inside Kaden, spiraling from his lips to his belly and lower still. He gasped at the sensation, his head falling back as Logan's mouth locked onto the sensitive skin at the base of his neck. He felt a tug in his groin at the feel of Logan's slick tongue flicking over his flesh. Logan's hands roamed down his back to slide beneath Kaden's shirt, the rough skin of his palms slid over his bare back, sending a shaft of desire through Kaden. Nothing else existed, just them and the fire rising higher with each tender kiss and soft caress. Logan lifted Kaden in his arms again, and carried him to the bed, carefully laying him down and leaning back to gaze at him. He perched on the edge of the bed, cupping Kaden's cheek and stroking the skin there with his thumb.

He helped the teenager remove his shirt, baring his upper body to Logan's parched gaze. Logan dropped light kisses along Kaden's collarbone, traveling lower to capture a stiff nub between his lips, tearing a gasp from Kaden. His tongue laved the nipple, swirling around the hard little button before he suckled slowly, enjoying the sounds issuing from the boy's throat. He moved his attentions to the other, running his hand down the muscles on Kaden's chest.

A split second of panic spiked inside Kaden when he felt Logan's hands working on the button and zipper of his jeans, but he buried it deep in his mind. He wanted this, and refused to allow the memories to ruin it for him. Pleasure zipped through him at the feel of the calloused palms on his skin, and then Logan carefully removed the last articles of clothing separating him from the cowboy. A flush invaded Kaden's cheeks at suddenly being so bare in front of Logan, but when he felt the bigger man tenderly slide his hands down his left leg and then up the right one, caressing and massaging as he moved, he forgot his embarrassment quickly. He sucked in a deep breath when the back of Logan's fingers brushed against his erect cock, and his eyes slid closed in rapture.

A cry escaped his lips at the feel of the wet, hot heat that closed around the tip of his shaft, and the cry faded into groans of lust as Logan sucked him deep inside his mouth. The feel of Logan's tongue on his cock sent bolts of lightning zipping up his spine. He'd never felt anything like it before. The cowboy flicked the tip of his tongue along the bottom of his stiff prick as Logan's mouth rose and fell on him. Kaden felt something spiraling inside of him, begging for release, and he let out several mewling cries, his hips jerking slightly. Logan pinned his hips to the bed and sucked harder and faster, coaxing Kaden to the edge. As Kaden reached that peak, Logan probed gently at the entrance to Kaden's body, feeling the tight heat that gripped his finger as the teenager's back arched from the bed, a cry of ecstasy resounding in the room. Warm liquid splashed into Logan's mouth, and he swallowed instinctively, moaning at the taste of Kaden's essence.

He continued to lap Kaden's softening flesh until no trace of his little one's orgasm remained, releasing it to fall back onto Kaden's soft belly. He licked his lips and moved up to rest beside Kaden, lazily trailing his fingers over the soft skin of the teen's chest. Kaden lay there in a daze. Never having believed another's touch could bring him such pleasure, it left him reeling. A multitude of emotions raced through him: happiness, wonder, and the most important one of all, love. He turned his head to gaze at Logan, his eyes glistening with tears. Logan frowned. "What's wrong?"

"N-nothing. I just never… knew it could feel so good. I've… never felt like that before," Kaden managed, his eyes lowering to lock onto the cowboy's broad chin.

Logan smirked in satisfaction, leaning forward to kiss Kaden's forehead. "Well, it's not over yet. That was only the appetizer." He slipped from the bed, smiling reassuringly at the hesitant expression on Kaden's face. He padded barefoot into the bathroom to get a condom and the small tube of KY Shea had passed to him in the kitchen a few days ago. He could still feel the heat that crawled up his neck when he'd seen the tube. She'd laughed uproariously at the discomfort on his face before slapping him on his shoulder and walking away.

He set them on the nightstand, and slowly removed his clothing, slipping back into the bed beside Kaden. "I'm going to let you control whatever we do, Kaden. It's up to you how far you want this to go."

Kaden's hand trembled as he reached out to place it lightly on the muscular chest, running his fingers experimentally over the tan flesh. The light dusting of blond hairs on Logan's chest tickled his palm, eliciting a small smile from Kaden. He sat up, moving closer to Logan's side, gazing down at him in wonder. Their skin contrasted deeply against one another. From his days spent in the sun, Logan's body was a dark tan, while Kaden's gleamed like white alabaster in the light thrown across the bed from the lamp on the nightstand. He ran the tip of one finger over the man's nipple, watching Logan's reaction and the way the man's lips parted on a soft sigh. He did it again, lingering this time. He wanted to make Logan feel as good as he had. Bending down, he took that little brown nub into his mouth, swiping his tongue over it. A groan rumbled in Logan's chest, causing the skin in his mouth to vibrate against his tongue.

He took his time, leisurely touching and exploring the man's body, learning the firm contours, and the velvety skin inside Logan's thighs. He found a birthmark in the shape of a strawberry on Logan's inner thigh, and it fascinated him so much that he couldn't help but taste it. Kaden tentatively licked at the smudge on his lover's body, enjoying the sound Logan made.

Sweat beaded on Logan's forehead as he strained to keep from grabbing Kaden and taking him roughly. The kid was driving him crazy with lust—the delicate, fluttery touches of his fingers, the tongue that now laved at the skin on his thigh, and the warm breath that passed over his swollen sac. "Kaden, you're driving me insane," he growled, arching his hips from the bed.

Kaden grinned, looking up at Logan from beneath his eyelashes. "But I like learning every inch of you. You're so beautiful."

For the first time in ages, Logan actually felt self-conscious and had to fight off a blush rising in his cheeks. But he quickly forgot his chagrin when Kaden's fingers wrapped around his aching shaft, and those slender fingers began to explore the silk-sheathed, engorged cock. Logan's breath hissed from his lungs when the kid tentatively swiped at the large tip with his tongue, tasting him. It took every ounce of willpower he possessed not to fill Kaden's mouth with his seed when the boy suddenly took him into his mouth and slid down to the bottom, taking him deep into his throat. It surprised him that the kid could take all of him so easily, and before he could explode at the erotic act, he lifted Kaden away from his dick and brought him up onto the bed beside him.

Logan fumbled for the tube of KY, his breathing heavy with desire and the strain of keeping himself in check. "Turn on your side facing away from me," he instructed calmly, and Kaden hesitantly rolled to his side.

A shudder wound its way through Kaden's body when he felt a large hand caressing his back, slipping down to grip his ass lightly. Kaden stifled a gasp when he felt Logan pressing a finger covered in a cold substance against his entrance. Terror rose to the surface, and he closed his eyes, praying it would recede as Logan began to push inside him. Once inside to the second knuckle, Logan retreated and pushed his finger back inside, repeating this until he felt Kaden begin to relax.

Adding a second finger to the first, he began to loosen Kaden's channel, scissoring his fingers and spreading him open. Panting gasps were coming from Kaden's mouth, and he bent forward to murmur into the teen's ear, "Are you all right?"

"Yes," Kaden sighed, pain and pleasure becoming one at the invasion of his body, but the pain had begun to fade away.

Two fingers became three, and Kaden began to push back on those fingers, his cock once again hard with need and dripping with wetness. Logan couldn't take any more and withdrew his fingers. He ripped open the condom wrapper, rolling it over his straining flesh before slathering it with lubricant. He felt Kaden tense anew when the head pushed against his hole, and he caressed the younger man's hip, soothing him as he began to push inside, his eyes locked on the sight of his thick cock slowly penetrating Kaden's body.

Kaden bit his lip as tears sprung into his eyes and a couple escaped to soak into the pillow beneath. It burned as he opened to the invasion, but it also felt good. The longer Logan remained inside of him, the more the pain dissipated. He instinctively huddled into Logan's chest, taking reassurance in the warmth at his back.

Logan stayed still, resisting the primal need to thrust in and out. He placed a tender kiss to Kaden's thin, pale shoulder. "Does it hurt?"

"No. It… feels… good," Kaden breathed, reaching back to grip Logan's hip, and arching his back.

The cowboy let out a small grunt at the way the snug entrance grew even tighter around him at the movement, and he began to thrust, pulling back until he remained partway inside Kaden and then shoving forward. He repositioned Kaden's leg until his knee rested against his thin chest, opening him wider for Logan. Logan lined his lover's shoulder and neck with kisses, carefully thrusting in and out of the hot canal gripping his cock. Kaden's slim fingers dug into his skin but it only added to the intense pleasure he felt.

"Kaden, I love you so much," Logan moaned, sinking his teeth lightly into the pale skin on Kaden's shoulder as he closed his eyes in ecstasy.

Heat spiraled higher inside Kaden, his stomach clenching almost painfully, and when Logan brushed against something deep inside him, he gave a small keening cry as the heat threatened to consume him. Their groans filled the room, sweat dampening their skin and the scent of sex heavy in the air as they undulated against each other. Kaden felt so hot, like his body had been consumed by fire, tiny flames licking at his skin, burning him deep inside. He could feel Logan inside him, filling him and emptying him again and again. The deeper Logan went, the better it felt. His own hips began to thrust back against Logan, increasing the pleasure tenfold.

"Kaden... ah... I need you to come for me, Kaden. Please... come for me," Logan bit out between clenched teeth, reaching around Kaden's body to grip the hard length of him, tugging on it in time with his own hard thrusts.

That was all that Kaden needed, sending him over the edge with a loud cry of Logan's name, his seed spilling across the sheets and Logan's fingers. Logan felt Kaden convulsing around his cock, milking him, and it sent him flying, his own fluids pumping into the latex sheathing his flesh. He roared through his climax, thrusting himself deep inside Kaden one last time before coming to a halt. They lay there, gasping for breath, and slowly descending back to earth.

Logan gripped the base of the condom, pulling out of Kaden's body to strip it from him and tie it closed before tossing it into the garbage can nearby. He turned back to pull Kaden into his arms, nuzzling at the teen's ear. He felt the trembling in Kaden's body, and tilted the boy's face in order to see his eyes. Tears were spilling down Kaden's cheeks, and Logan made a sound of alarm. "Kaden? Did I hurt you? Or scare you?" he asked in a panic, sitting up to gather Kaden into his lap.

Kaden couldn't respond. Words were lost to him. He shook his head profusely. He wrapped his arms around Logan's neck and held on tight to keep from flying apart. That had been incredible. Nothing had prepared him for it to be that way, and he felt cherished and loved by Logan. His own heart swelled up inside his chest, pounding hard and fast. No matter what happened, he loved the big, strong cowboy and nothing would ever change that. Once he'd managed to bring himself under control, giving an occasional hiccup, Kaden lifted his head to flash Logan a watery smile. "I didn't mean to cry all over you."

Logan wiped at the boy's tears and asked, "What was that all about? You had me scared. I thought I'd hurt you or frightened you."

"No. I'm sorry. I just never knew it could feel like that." Wonder and awe rang out in his voice. "And to be connected to you in such an intimate way was the most incredible thing I've ever felt, Logan. And it made me realize… how much I love you."

Logan jerked slightly in his embrace, and Kaden knew he'd surprised his lover by declaring his love for him. His eyes met Logan's, and the pure love shining out of the emerald depths stole his breath away. "I thought you'd never say it," Logan exhaled, kissing Kaden's cheeks, eyelids, forehead, and lastly his lips, drawing out the sweet kiss for what could have been forever, but Kaden gave himself up to it, showing Logan he no longer feared him.

They somehow managed to slip beneath the quilt, wrapped up in each other's arms. Kaden fell asleep first, his head resting on Logan's shoulder. Logan stared down at Kaden, astounded that the boy had admitted his own feelings for him. He pressed a kiss to Kaden's forehead before drifting into a deep, untroubled sleep.

When Logan awoke, Kaden was already up and downstairs making breakfast for the men. He yawned and stretched, his lips curved into a giant grin. He felt wonderful! Kaden's words last night couldn't have made him happier. His breath hitched at the thought of such a beautiful young man as Kaden loving him. If someone had told him a year ago that he would find himself in love with another man, and that the man would love him back, he would have scoffed at the idea and possibly kicked someone's ass. But now he thanked God for bringing Kaden into his life, making him believe in love again. Humming softly, still smiling, Logan climbed out of bed to take a quick shower and dress.

Kaden finished up the eggs, placing them on the huge platter, and brought it into the dining room. His eyes sparkled brightly, happily, a warm glow radiating from deep inside him. Placing the last platter of food on the sideboard, he saw the dining room door open and Shea sneaking in, a guilty expression on her face. She saw him and came to a halt, her face chagrined. He smiled at her. "Good morning, Shea."

She studied him for a split second, and then her face brightened and a wide, satisfied smirk spread across her lips. "You're awfully cheerful for this early in the morning, Kaden. Something happen?"

A blush worked its way over his cheeks, and he grinned at her, but didn't offer her an explanation. Though he had little doubt that she couldn't see it in his eyes and on his face, that warm after-sex glow that you get when you've been really satisfied. She had the same one on her face as well. Kaden winked at her and darted back into the kitchen to start washing pots and wipe down the counters. Logan caught Shea on the way up to her room, and he berated her angrily, to which she replied cheekily, "Don't even try it, bro. I know what you and Kaden were up to last night. It's so obvious on your face and his. So don't be yelling at me for something you yourself are guilty of." And then she disappeared into her bedroom.

Logan shook his head and heaved a deep sigh, knowing he couldn't deny the truth of her words, and he couldn't keep the grin off his face. He trotted down the stairs, stepping into the kitchen to find Kaden leaning against the sink, washing dishes. He walked up behind him, sliding his arms around his waist. "Good morning, my love," he whispered into the soft pink ear.

Kaden sighed in contentment, leaning back against Logan. "Good morning, Logan."

"You smell good. I didn't even hear you get up to take a shower," Logan told him crossly, but without any true anger behind the statement.

"I went down to my own room to shower," Kaden replied. "I didn't want to wake you."

"Well, that room won't be yours much longer. In fact, tonight you'll be moving into mine," Logan growled softly into Kaden's ear, smirking at the pink tinge that stained Kaden's cheeks. "I don't want to spend another night alone."

Kaden turned in Logan's arms, gazing up into the man's face. "Are you sure? I don't want to crowd you."

"Of course, I'm sure. I am the one who suggested it, aren't I?" the man demanded fiercely. "Besides, I could never feel crowded by you."

"Okay."

"Good. Then tonight we'll bring your stuff upstairs. Now, let's sit down and eat. I can hear the men coming."

Kaden couldn't remember ever being this happy. Unable to stop smiling, he watched Logan and the men head out to start their day. They had started on the last section, and it wouldn't be long until the roundup had finished. Shea never came down to breakfast, crashing in her plush bed after a long night of loving. If she'd had any idea of the events that would unfold that morning, she'd have been downstairs with her daddy's shotgun, waiting. Kaden happily hummed to himself as he finished washing the dishes and began to dry them. So lost in his thoughts, he didn't hear the dining room door open and shut, or the sound of booted feet creeping across the floor boards, trying to be as quiet as possible. The sound of a boot on the doorjamb between the kitchen and dining room alerted him to someone's presence, and Kaden turned his head with a smile already forming, wondering if Logan had forgotten something, but that smile never made it to its full potential because the sight of the person behind him brought him to an abrupt and shattering halt.

CHAPTER 15

FRANKLIN stood there, an evil, nasty grin on his face. He had a wild, glazed look in his slimy hazel eyes, and Kaden almost gagged at the distinct smell of alcohol. Kaden shrank back against the sink when the man advanced several feet.

"You little bashtard. You're the reashon my wife left me and took my little girlsh with her," the man slurred, moving closer until he stood directly in front of Kaden.

Kaden opened his mouth to scream in the hope that Shea would hear, but the man slammed his fist into the side of Kaden's face, knocking the breath from him and sending him reeling into the nearby stove. Suddenly the man's hands were everywhere, ripping at his clothing, and this time he did cry out in fear. Franklin's hand clamped down on his mouth, muffling his cries, and he struggled to undress the kid with one hand. Kaden bit down hard, causing Franklin to shriek in pain. "You little shit!" He grabbed Kaden by the throat and flung him into the kitchen table, one of the chairs splintered.

Part of the leg speared through Kaden's shoulder, ripping a scream from him before Franklin picked him up again and tossed him bodily into a china hutch that lined one wall. The glass doors shattered, dishes smashed, and the wood of the doors rained down in pieces. Kaden grunted at the hot searing pain in his lower back. He collapsed onto the ground, gasping in agony, tears streaming down his face. The only thoughts he had were for Logan and what he would suffer through afterward. Franklin loomed over him, a smug smirk lining his lips. "You're mine now." Franklin picked him up from the ground, uncaring of the blood that pooled on the floor beneath Kaden's still frame, and hurling the teenager down belly first onto the kitchen table, leaving his legs hanging to the floor.

It hurt. More than any of the wounds his stepfather had inflicted. Kaden wanted to run, to get away, but he couldn't move his legs, his arms flailing uselessly. Tears blurred his vision further when he felt his jeans being ripped down his legs, baring him to the disgusting man about to rape him.

"No… please, no," he begged as he felt the man's cock touching his entrance, and suddenly Franklin vanished. He could hear yelling and fists hitting flesh. Kaden's vision swam, and his consciousness faded, taking him deep down into the warm depths. Before it could claim him completely, his last thought once again returned to Logan.

Logan had returned to the house to get the first-aid kit, since one of the men had torn open his shoulder on some barb wire. He'd heard the sound of glass shattering and yelling coming from the house. Panic had torn through him as he raced from the truck into the house. That's when he'd seen Kaden covered in blood, and the son of a bitch Franklin standing behind him, ready to rape him. He threw his body at the man, rage boiling over inside him at the way the bastard had hurt his Kaden. His fist landed with a satisfying crunch upon the man's face, breaking his nose. Franklin fell back drunkenly, glaring at Logan and holding his nose. Logan again lunged at the man, raining fist after fist of anger down on him. "Oh, my God!" he heard Shea cry from behind him, and it brought him back to earth.

Franklin lay unconscious beneath him, blood spilling from his split lips and nose. Logan stood, and he rushed over to Kaden, almost crying at the sight of the boy lying there. He hurriedly pulled up the kid's jeans, and took in the situation. Swearing profusely, he yelled at Shea to get her attention. "Call the sheriff, *now*! Tell him to get over here and arrest this sack of shit before I kill him. And once you do that, radio Charlie and tell him to send some of the men back here to watch this bastard until the sheriff gets here."

Logan tied Franklin tightly to a chair, making sure the knots were secure before he carefully picked up Kaden and carried him to his truck, trying to keep from jarring him. Kaden was covered in so much blood, and his skin looked so pale. "Don't you dare leave me, Kaden. Not after I just found you. Do you hear me?" he snarled fiercely, covering Kaden's prone form with the blanket from the day of their picnic before starting the truck and tearing out of the ranch driveway.

He raced toward town, praying that God would keep his little one safe until he could get him to a hospital. He breathed a small sigh of relief when the town came into view, and he slammed on the brakes in front of the clinic, leaving the truck running and carefully lifting Kaden from the truck. Blood covered the front of his own clothes, and the nurse screamed when he burst into the clinic. "Where's the doc? Please, Betty! He's dying!" Logan wasn't even aware of the tears that spilled from his eyes or of the absolute terror on his face.

The doctor rushed out of the back room, where he'd been examining another patient, and indicated for Logan to bring Kaden into one of the examining rooms. Without looking, the doctor shouted at his nurse to call for a MedEvac chopper before trying to stop the blood flow. He didn't want to remove the large piece of glass that was wedged into the boy's lower left back for fear that he'd cause more damage than good.

It took fifteen excruciatingly long minutes for the MedEvac to arrive, during which time Logan held onto Kaden's hand, refusing to let him go. "Stay with me, Kaden. Please!" His voice sounded hoarse from trying to stem his tears and holding in his anguish.

The chopper blades were loud above their heads as they soared toward the hospital, Logan whispering in Kaden's ear the entire way there. "I won't let you go. I'll follow you to the heights of heaven and the depths of hell to fight God and the devil himself to keep you!"

The moment that they reached the hospital, they whisked Kaden away, leaving Logan standing in the hallway staring after the doctors and nurses rushing the younger man toward surgery. He hadn't felt such blinding numbness since he'd found his parents in the kitchen all those years ago. He dropped to his knees right there in the middle of the crowded corridor, burying his face in his hands. Tears spilled over now, and great shudders began to wrack the cowboy's shoulders. A warm hand settled on one of his shoulders and another on his arm, helping him up from the floor to the waiting room. "I'm sure he'll be fine, sir. Our doctors are some of the best in the world. Just have faith," the nurse murmured soothingly, patting his shoulder before leaving him to his private grief.

Shea arrived an hour later, rushing into the emergency room. "Can someone tell me if Kaden James is okay?"

Logan heard her voice but didn't look up. The woman at the nurse's station pointed into the waiting room where he sat, and Shea rushed to his side, sinking down into the chair next to him. "Is he going to be okay?" she asked, her eyes pleading that he tell her yes.

"I don't know," he replied gruffly. "They've been in there for over an hour, and they haven't told me anything. Oh God, Shea. If he...." He trailed off, his voice cracking and choking in his throat.

Shea gathered her brother into her arms, rubbing his back comfortingly. "Shh. He'll be fine, Logan. He's strong and a fighter. And he loves you very much. He won't leave you."

Several hours later, Logan paced back and forth in the waiting room, his eyes blazing angrily. "Why the hell haven't they come out yet? How long can it take, damn it!"

"Sit down, Logan. I'm sure they are doing the best they can," Shea said wearily, rubbing her eyes tiredly. Her brother had steadily grown more and more restless as the hours drifted by. "No news is good news, bro."

Another hour passed before a doctor came out of the doors, sighing tiredly, his face haggard from the long hours in the operating room. He stepped into the waiting room. "Is there anyone here for Kaden James?"

Logan stood up from where he'd been perched on the edge of his chair. "Is he going to be all right?"

"We can't be sure yet. We removed the large section of glass embedded in his lower back, but it nicked his spinal cord. We repaired as much of the damage as possible, but we don't know if he'll ever be able to walk again. Right now he's in recovery, and in stable condition. The next few days will tell us more, and once he's awake, we can establish if he will be confined to a wheelchair or not."

Shea let out a gasp at the doctor's words, her hand covering her mouth and her eyes shimmering with unshed tears. Logan's hands fisted at his sides, and he demanded, "When can we see him?"

"A nurse will take you to him once he's out of recovery." The doctor turned on his heel and left, his heart heavy with the bad news he'd just delivered. It always saddened him not to be able to offer hope to the relatives and loved ones of his patients.

Logan kept his head tilted down, his eyes closed, and he tried to keep from screaming in rage and anguish. The boy had already been through so much, and now to find out that he might never walk again. If Kaden died, he'd rip that bastard limb from limb and feed him to the coyotes. He heard the sounds of soft weeping, low murmurs of voices, and the sounds of staff being paged over the PA system echoing around him. The smell of antiseptic stung his nostrils when he breathed deeply. If he had known that Franklin would try something like this, he never would have left Kaden alone.

His mind flashed back to the night before, the flushed look of pleasure on Kaden's face, the sound of the boy's whimpers and sighs, and the feel of his bare skin against his. The teen's confession of love and the shy smile on those beautiful lips all washed over him, almost sending him to his knees in pain. *You have to live, Kaden. You just have to.*

Another couple of hours passed before the nurse came to get him and Shea, leading them to the intensive care unit and the room that Kaden lay in, still as death. Shea started to sob, reaching out to brush Kaden's hair back from his forehead. Logan leaned over and kissed Kaden's lips. They were cool to the touch, almost as if there were no life in them, and it made his heart pound in fear. The monitors nearby beeped steadily indicating the teen's heartbeat, and Logan grabbed a chair nearby to settle down next to Kaden, picking up the boy's hand and holding it to his cheek.

Kaden's skin looked so pale against the sheets. There was no flush of pleasure, no sparkle of life, no husky laughter from the boy's mouth. Tears stung Logan's eyes yet again, and he closed them tightly, squeezing them shut and praying that God would hear him. He couldn't lose him.

Logan lost track of time and days as Kaden remained in a

coma-like state. The doctors didn't seem concerned, stating that after a traumatic and damaging event the mind shut down while the body healed. Logan barely slept, never ate, and just waited. He waited for any sign of Kaden coming back to him. Shea brought him some clothes, updating him about the happenings at the ranch. The men were getting along fine without him, Charlie had taken over, and they'd already started bringing the rest of the cattle in for branding and gelding. It wouldn't be long before they were sent out to auction. Nothing mattered to Logan anymore, except the boy who lay unresponsive in the bed day after day.

Shea reprimanded him for not eating, leaving the room to go get him something from the cafeteria. Logan turned back to the bed, picking up his vigil once more. "Please, Kaden, open your eyes for me. I need to see those beautiful purple eyes of yours. I need to see that adorable smile I love so much." His words were always the same. Telling Kaden he loved him and needed him, begging the boy not to leave him.

A change came about a week after the teen was hospitalized: his hand twitched, the one Logan held. Logan looked at him in hope and eagerness, pleading for Kaden to wake up. Logan watched as Kaden's eyelids slowly lifted, revealing dull violet orbs. "L-Logan," Kaden whispered, bewildered and confused.

"Kaden. Oh, thank God!" Logan surged out of his seat, leaning over to hug Kaden carefully and press a gentle kiss to the teen's lips.

"Where am I?" Kaden asked, still unsure as to what had really happened.

"Livingston Memorial Hospital. You were admitted due to massive blood loss and injuries. You don't remember?"

Kaden searched his mind for what had happened. It took a minute, but then his eyes widened in remembrance, and tears welled up "He… he was going to…."

"Shh. It's all right. He didn't get the chance. He's rotting in jail right now. And I swear on everything I am that he will never touch you again." Logan tenderly caressed Kaden's cheek, a small encouraging smile curving his lips.

The doctor came in then and realized Kaden had awakened. He spent some time doing tests and asking Kaden questions. He informed him about his injuries and the surgery, as well as the fact that he might not be able to walk again. The kind doctor also gently suggested that Kaden might think about possibly speaking with a psychiatrist regarding his previous abuse and the current situation. Kaden sat there in stunned silence, staring at the doctor as though he'd suddenly grown another head. His eyes moved to Logan, and the pain he saw in the emerald orbs he adored. Once the doctor left, Logan returned to his side, holding his hand again. "Don't you dare get upset, Kaden. You'll walk again, and no matter what happens, I love you, and that will never change. Do you hear me?"

He'd seen the shift in the teenager's features as the doctor spoke, and knew the thoughts going through Kaden's mind. That he was going to be a burden on them, but he would never let Kaden leave him. "I won't let you go, no matter what. I have faith in you. You will be able to walk," Logan said fiercely.

Kaden gave him a strained look, turned his head away, and began to cry. Why did God do this to him? Why wasn't he ever allowed to be happy? He felt the big cowboy slide onto the bed beside him, gingerly moving him into his arms and holding him. "I love you, Kaden. That's all that matters. Hush, now. Get some sleep, and we'll take it one day at a time, baby." His tears slowly subsided, and he drifted back to sleep, exhausted from emotional upheaval and the worry that plagued him.

The first to wake, Kaden lay there, resting close to Logan's large, warm body, and stared up at the ceiling. The doctor had said he'd be back by this morning to check for any sensation in his legs, and to make sure that everything seemed to be healing all right with his back and shoulder. His eyes flooded again, and he stifled a sob as tears trickled over one by one. Silently, they treaded their way down his cheeks, dripping into his hair and soaking into the pillow. He turned his head to look at Logan through blurry eyes. His handsome face had slackened in sleep, his lips parted, and his long black lashes rested against his cheeks. Kaden couldn't believe that such a beautiful man would really want someone like him, with his scars and now possibly paralyzed.

He started in surprise when Logan's sleep-coarse voice issued from his lips. "Stop thinking what you're thinking, little one. You aren't going anywhere, no matter what the outcome." Those green eyes slowly opened, still glazed slightly from sleep, but Kaden's breath hitched in his throat when he saw the depth of love and affection shining out at him. Logan smiled sleepily and lifted his hand to cup Kaden's cheek, running a thumb over it. "You don't understand at all, do you? I love you, and no matter if you lose an arm, a leg, grow a second head, or whatever, that will never change."

"But—" the teenager went to protest, but Logan stopped him with his lips, crushing Kaden's beneath his. Logan's slick, wet tongue flowed along Kaden's bottom lip.

"I love you." Logan kissed him again. "I love you." And he kissed him again. "I… love… you."

Kaden couldn't resist smiling between kisses, wrapping his arms around Logan's neck. The sound of a voice clearing in the doorway brought their avid attention away from each other. Kaden blushed hiding his face in Logan's chest, but Logan merely grinned and greeted the doctor. The man moved closer to the bed. "Good morning, Kaden. How are we feeling today? Any pain?"

"No," the teenager muttered, warily watching the doctor approach.

"Good. Now, Mr. Michaels, if you would be so kind as to give me some space, I need to do a few small tests." The doctor hinted at Logan to move off the bed, and Kaden watched him with wide eyes. Logan moved to stand nearby, watching intently.

The doctor pulled the sheet back, revealing Kaden's legs, and he touched his right leg. "Do you feel that?"

Kaden shook his head in the negative. The doctor moved to his feet, trying to tickle Kaden and intently watched for a response. "And that?" Another shake of the head answered his question. The doctor made a few notes on his board before picking up Kaden's right leg and resting his foot on his shoulder near his ear. He ran his fingers along Kaden's leg and up to his thigh. "Anything there?"

A sad look entered Kaden's eyes as he shook his head no. The doctor did several other tests before he finished and placed Kaden's leg back on the bed, covering him with the sheet. "How's it look, Doc?" Logan asked, immediately stepping back to the side of the bed to pick up Kaden's hand.

"Well, the good news is that, even though Kaden did not feel anything personally, his skin twitched several times. That's a very good sign. If his legs were entirely paralyzed, there would be no response in any form. Now, we'll have to get you started on physical therapy once those wounds heal and see where it goes from there. Don't lose hope, Kaden. If you lose hope, it will impede your recovery and the possibility that you may be able to walk again." The doctor patted Kaden's ankle before exiting the room.

Logan felt relief at the doctor's words, and reached out to grab the chair nearby to pull it closer. He settled his long frame in it, never releasing Kaden's hand. Kaden lay there without speaking, and struggled to move his toes. They did not respond in any way to his attempt to move them. A nurse came in a short time later to bring him his breakfast which Logan forced him to eat most of. The big cowboy made it hard to be depressed. Talking to him, constantly telling him that he loved him, and more.

Three days after Kaden woke up, Logan had to return to the ranch. "As soon as roundup is finished, I will be back. Shea will be staying here with you during the days. And I'll call you every night. Don't go giving the nurses a hard time about eating, Kaden." The big man gave him a stern look, to which Kaden smirked slightly because he knew it didn't contain any real anger. "They've had express instructions to call me if you do, and I'll be back up before you can spit to make sure you do."

"Yes, sir!" Kaden saluted him, having a hard time keeping the smile from his lips.

Logan laughed, leaning down to kiss him again. "Don't ever forget that I love you, Kaden. No matter what. Do you hear me? Please do your best to get well. I want to take you home soon. Promise me?"

The emerald eyes hovering above his were concerned, affectionate, and pleading. Home. That word echoed in his mind once Logan had left with his promise to try his hardest to stay positive. The cowboy considered him part of their family, and he kept trying to remind himself that if the situations were reversed, he would still feel the same about Logan.

CHAPTER 16

A SOUND brought his head around, and he saw a little girl standing in the doorway of his room. Adorable, she had big blue eyes, bright red curls, and wore a hospital gown while clutching a ragged teddy bear. "Hi," she said solemnly, staying close to the doorway.

"Hi," Kaden responded, curious as to where the little girl had come from.

"Are you sick?" she asked.

That brought him up short. What did he tell her? He supposed the truth never hurt. So with a deep breath, he said, "I guess you could say that. I was hurt very badly, and my legs aren't working right now."

The girl edged into the room a little farther, still clutching the teddy bear. "I'm sick."

"I'm very sorry to hear that. What's wrong?"

She moved closer to him and climbed up into the chair near the bed, folding her legs underneath her. The air of innocence around the little girl made it almost hurt for Kaden to look at her. He smiled encouragingly at her. She grinned back suddenly, nearly blinding him with the brilliance. "The doctor says I gots cancer, in my head." She pointed at the shiny red curls.

Kaden's breath caught, and he felt sadness fill him that such a beautiful little girl should have to suffer like that. It astounded him that the little girl didn't seem to be sad or upset about being sick. It humbled him. "I'm Kaden. What's your name?"

"Becca Thompson." She introduced herself proudly and stuck out her tiny hand in greeting.

He smiled as he engulfed the small appendage in between his own, marveling at the difference in size. "It's nice to meet you, Becca. Where's your mommy?"

"She's in heaven with my Grammy. My daddy had to work so he can pay for the medicine to fix me." Her blue eyes were guileless, and it made Kaden feel ashamed about the way he'd been acting. It made him realize that he was lucky to be alive.

"I'm sorry to hear that. My mom's there too. Along with my dad."

"You don't have a mommy or daddy?" Becca asked, her eyes wide. "Then who takes care of you?"

Kaden couldn't help but smile as he thought of Logan and Shea. "My friends take care of me."

"Oh. That's good. Can I be your friend too?" the little girl asked timidly, almost seemingly afraid that he would reject her. Kaden nodded and she grinned, bouncing on the chair.

"There you are, Becca!" A young woman in a candy-striper outfit stepped into the room. "I've been looking all over for you." She scolded the little girl gently, giving Kaden an apologetic smile. "She got away from me."

"That's all right. If it's all right with you and, of course, her father, I wouldn't mind her coming to visit whenever she wants," Kaden encouraged, wanting to be around the little girl and help her if he could.

Becca started chattering to the candy striper eagerly as they left, the little girl giving him a small kiss on the cheek before grabbing the woman's hand and allowing her to lead her from the room. Kaden lay back against the pillow with a sigh. It didn't seem fair that such a beautiful, innocent child should be afflicted by such an illness. It made him want to do whatever he could to get better so that he could help her. But the doctor had said that physical therapy would have to wait until his wounds had healed for the most part, which could take weeks. He grimaced, looking around the sterile room. The flowers from Logan and the balloons from Shea offered the only splash of color. His eyes settled on the various colors of the daisies, pansies, and daffodils that were in the bunch. They were beautiful, and he felt his lips curve up slightly in the corners at the thought of the man who'd given them to him.

By the time Kaden healed enough to allow physical therapy, he'd grown impatient and ansty. The little girl came to visit him almost every day, telling him about herself and her friends. He told her some of his childhood, nothing of his abuse, but he did speak about his mom. Becca gave him hope and made him see that he had a long life ahead of him, so he needed to enjoy it and live life to the fullest. Logan had met Becca one day, and Kaden couldn't help but break down to Logan after she left, telling the cowboy about the girl's illness. Logan had comforted him, and held him while he cried, whispering soothing things to him.

Kaden was watching a comedy show on TV when the physical therapist came in. A very large, very tall man pushed a wheelchair into the room, accompanied by the doctor. "Good morning, Kaden. How are we feeling today?"

"Good." Kaden eyed the big man warily, watching while the man locked the wheels on the chair and approached his bed.

"This is Sam. He's going to be your physical therapist while we try to get those legs of yours working again." The doctor made some notations on a chart for Kaden and then exited the room, leaving them alone.

Kaden watched the man nervously. "Hello, Kaden. I hope that we can be friends while we work at getting those legs of yours moving again." Sam smiled, sensing the teen's trepidation.

Sam, almost two inches taller than Logan, had a broad smile, big muscles, dark-auburn hair, and twinkling green eyes. The eyes reminded him slightly of Logan's, and Kaden felt himself relaxing slightly. "Now, I need to pick you up to put you in the wheelchair, all right?" Kaden tensed again when Sam slid one arm under his knees and the other under his back before hefting him up against his chest.

Sweat beaded on Kaden's forehead as he tried to control the panic flowing through him. Sam settled him gently into the wheelchair, unlocked the wheels, and started rolling him from the room. The large man began to chat easily to him on their way to the elevator, urging Kaden to answer him. By the time they got to the physical therapy ward, Kaden started smiling and laughing, looking up at the taller man when they stopped.

The therapy began slowly, Sam only putting him through about an hour's worth of movements. Kaden still felt nothing, but he pushed his despair from his mind, trying to remind himself that even if he couldn't walk again, Logan would be there for him, no matter what. Exhaustion nipped at him by the end of the session, and his head dipped close to his chest when they entered his hospital room. Sam had picked him up to put in the bed when the cowboy arrived, stopping abruptly at the sight of another man with his hands on Kaden. "Who are you?" Logan demanded, glaring at the man.

"I'm Sam, Kaden's physical therapist. You must be Logan." Sam approached the cowboy, sticking out his hand to shake.

Touch Me Gently

Logan carefully grasped the paw in front of him, still angry at the thought of this man touching his little one. But he couldn't do anything about it because this man would help Kaden walk again. He quickly let the man's hand go, moving over to Kaden's side and dropping a kiss on the boy's temple. "How are you feeling? And how did the first session go?"

Kaden launched into an animated description, neither of them noticing when Sam slipped from the room. Their eyes were locked on each other's, and Kaden instinctively reached for Logan's hand the second the cowboy had stepped up to his bed. It made Logan feel good to know that Kaden still wanted him near, and he smiled indulgently as the teenager talked, brushing his fingers over the side of Kaden's neck. "It sounds like you had a good day, then. That's good. I'm glad to hear that. I am so happy to see you smile, Kaden."

"I'm glad you're here, Logan. I've missed you." Kaden leaned into Logan's hand, closing his eyes and sighing contently. "I can't wait until I can go home. How's everything at the ranch? Has Shea poisoned anyone yet?" Shea had taken over cooking meals for the regular hands now that the ranch had gone back to its normal routine.

"No, she hasn't poisoned anyone yet. But I'll be sure to let her know your faith in her," Logan said dryly. "The food's not half-bad. She's been following the recipes from the books, and some of the ones you wrote down for her. It's nothing like yours, but once you're home and well, we can rotate the cooking duties. You'll have enough to do when you get home that I don't want all your attention on food."

Kaden gave him a quizzical look. "What do you mean by I'll have enough to do when I get home?"

A lusty shine entered Logan's eyes, and the big cowboy leaned down to whisper close to his ear, "Once you're home, I'm

177

not letting you out of the bedroom for a week. So you'd better be prepared to be in bed 'recovering' for a while." A breathy sigh issued from Kaden's lips, and his cheeks grew heated, not just with embarrassment but also from anticipation.

The physical therapy continued, Kaden spending most of his time with Sam over the following weeks. There hadn't been any results reached, no response to the therapy, and Kaden began to get discouraged. Becca visited less and less, becoming sicker and weaker as time went by. She'd grown very pale and unable to sit up for long periods of time. Now Kaden visited her instead. He would read stories to her or make up his own, trying to amuse her and see her smile, making faces while telling the story and using different voices for the characters. The father came by only once during the time Kaden visited, and the man acted very cold toward his daughter. It made his heart ache for the little girl.

The house of cards they'd built around each other as friends came tumbling down one day when Kaden went to visit her, only to find that she'd gotten very sick over night, vomiting up blood and losing consciousness. Kaden waited anxiously by her side, praying that God would help her.

"If you don't start trying harder, Kaden, you'll be stuck in a wheelchair for the rest of your life! Do you want that?" Sam glared at Kaden, at the boy sitting mutely, unmoving and uncaring, in the pool before him. They'd been working for almost thirty minutes, and Kaden remained stubbornly unenthusiastic and spaced out.

Kaden stared at Sam, battling the tears that always seemed to be just beneath the surface these days. Still in a coma, the doctors said it would be unlikely for Becca to come out of it. For the past week, he had been at her bedside almost constantly, talking to her and encouraging her to get better. His own depression kept coming forth, dampening his once almost blinding spirit toward getting better. Sam noticed it getting increasingly worse over the past few days, and he knew the reason why, but it frustrated him that the teenager wasn't using the situation to push himself harder. It had been almost four months since Kaden's accident, and his legs still hadn't responded, no matter how hard they worked. "Do you want to have someone help you do everything for the rest of your life? Now start working!" Sam used a harsh tone in the hopes of getting through to Kaden.

"I don't feel like it today," he replied listlessly, his eyes dull and lifeless.

"That's too bad! Because you're going to do it whether you like it or not. Now push!" Sam picked up Kaden's right leg and bent the knee in toward his thin chest.

Kaden sighed and willed his leg to push toward Sam, almost crying out when pain shot up through his body as his leg shoved forward, forcing the man's arms backward. "Excellent," Sam cried. "Again!"

"It hurts!" Kaden exclaimed, sweat popping out along his forehead, and he gritted his teeth. The physical therapist pushed his knee to his chest again, and Kaden felt a little less pain as he did it again, and again. Hope spread through his mind, body, and heart as it became easier to move the leg. Sam laid his right leg back down gently, and moved to his left leg, forcing him to repeat the same movements.

Finally the man let him rest, and Kaden's chest heaved from the deep breaths he took, his jaw aching from his teeth being clenched for so long. "This is great progress, Kaden! We'll do it again tomorrow." Sam helped him from the pool, lifting him up and taking him into the changing room, where he helped change him back to the shirt and sweatpants that Logan had brought him from home.

Maybe if he could walk again then Becca could get better. He prayed that God would help her, bring her back out of the coma, and help her get well. He promised to try harder in his own efforts if the Man above would just grant him this one wish. He could barely keep his head up as Sam wheeled him back to his room and moved him to the bed. Sleep claimed him for several hours, and when he woke Logan sat in the chair beside the bed reading a book. "Logan," he rasped, his voice still husky from sleep.

"You're awake." Logan smiled, marking his page in the book and setting it on the table near him. He stood and moved closer to the bed, leaning over to kiss Kaden briefly, running his tongue over the boy's smooth lips. He nuzzled at Kaden's neck for a few seconds before pulling away and smiling down at him. "Sam told me about your progress today. I'm so happy for you!"

Kaden felt tears welling up in his eyes as the thought of Becca came back to him. Logan looked at him in alarm. "What's wrong?"

Words tumbled out of him before he could stop them, and moments later he found himself gathered close to Logan's chest, being soothed and comforted. "Sometimes life deals us a hand that isn't always the easiest. And I'm sure God will do His best to help her if He can, but if she is meant to be with Him, then that is where she belongs. Work hard to get better so that when she comes out of the coma, you can help her get well, Kaden. I'm sure she'll be happy to see you walking again, and it will give her encouragement to get better too."

Lying there weakly, Kaden listened to Logan's heartbeat beneath his ear, and wondered at how his life had changed so much since he'd met this man. "Logan?"

"Hmm?" the cowboy sighed, just enjoying the feel of Kaden in his arms. He couldn't wait to bring him home. He missed the boy's light and laughter in his house. It made the old ranch house seem sterile without him.

"I love you." Kaden's voice was strong and even as he spoke, ensuring that Logan knew he told the truth.

Logan tenderly brushed a lock of Kaden's dark hair behind his ear, bending his head close to the pale ear to murmur, "I love you, too, my little one."

Warmth spread throughout Kaden's body, bringing with it a sense of safety and peace. Something he hadn't felt in a very long time. Logan shifted so that he could lie down beside him, and they cuddled, holding one another and relishing being together. No matter what had happened, Logan still loved him, and it left him breathless. The trouble he'd caused since his arrival, the panic attacks, the frustration that Logan must have felt when they had only kissed and hugged—yet nothing seemed to make the big cowboy think less of him or love him any less. Maybe he was worth loving, and maybe, just maybe, he could finally be happy.

Becca's condition didn't change, pushing Kaden to work harder and harder. He also begged for God to hear his words as he prayed at her bedside. Such a beautiful little girl, full of life and spirit, didn't deserve to have her already short life cut shorter. Within weeks of his first bit of progress, he started using crutches to get around. Eventually, he graduated to a cane and limping as he walked. Each step caused him pain but it gave him hope, for himself and for the little red-headed girl that he'd come to love in such a short time. The doctors were doing as much as they could to help her, but it didn't appear as though it would be enough. The rest would be up to God.

The day before Kaden was scheduled to go home to the ranch, Becca came to him in his dreams. She wore a white gown, her curls shiny and bright around her head, holding the hand of a woman he had never seen before. She smiled at him and blew him a kiss, beaming up at the woman beside her. Even though he couldn't speak, he could hear words coming from the little girl, though he wasn't sure if he understood them. Suddenly he knew the woman holding Becca's hand had to be her mother. The moment he woke, he started to cry, big gulping sobs. She was gone. He knew it in his heart as he slowly sat up, pulling the covers back and lowering his feet to the floor. He grabbed his cane and limped from his room, making his way over to the children's ward. As he approached her room, he saw the candy striper, Sandy, coming from Becca's room, crying. She looked up at him, and her face told him the answer he already knew.

Kaden walked toward the girl, and they hugged each other as he gazed in on Becca's empty bed. Even though it broke his heart, he knew Becca was with her mother and no longer in pain. There had been such warmth in the light that surrounded the little girl and such peace in her eyes as she'd smiled at him. He breathed in deeply, willing his tears away because Becca would be mad if he gave in to his sadness. He smiled as he remembered the day that she had started getting angry with him because he hadn't been willing to do his physical therapy. Her eyes had sparked with temper, and she'd started demanding that he get out of bed, telling him that he wasn't allowed to not try. That he had to try for her, because who else would take her to the park while her daddy was working? It had chased away his depression, leaving him with the willingness to try again.

Kaden stayed quiet the next morning when Logan came to get him, and it immediately attracted the cowboy's concern. "What's wrong, Kaden? Did something happen?"

A sad smile pushed at the corner of his lips, not quite reaching his eyes. "Becca passed away last night."

"Oh, Kaden." Engulfed in the cowboy's strong embrace, Logan held Kaden tightly to his warm body. Fingers combed through his dark hair, and one of the large hands rubbed his back soothingly. "I'm so sorry."

"It's okay. I know she's with her mother and that she's happy. She came to me in my dreams last night. To tell me not to be sad and that she was proud of me for walking again." Kaden wrapped his arms around Logan's waist, holding on tight. "I want to go see her dad. To tell him that she's going to be okay."

Logan pulled back to look down at the sad teenager, but there were no tears in the gaze looking up at him, just acceptance and grief. "All right, I'll take your things to the car, and meet you at the front entrance."

Kaden nodded, leaving the room and moving as quickly as he could to the Pediatrics ward. A sense of rightness about what he intended to do settled itself into his heart, burrowing deeply. The father sat in a chair outside Becca's room, hunched over with his face buried in his hands. As Kaden approached, the man looked up and fresh tears spilled over again when he spotted the teenage boy who'd been his daughter's friend. Kaden lowered himself beside the man, wrapping his arms around the shaking shoulders. Grief could make the largest man in the world seem so small under the weight of it. "My little girl is gone. She's gone," the father wailed, rocking back and forth.

"Becca's going to be okay, Mr. Thompson. She's together with her mom and at peace," Kaden said quietly, trying to get the man to hear his words. "I know it in my heart, and I know she's happy where she is. She will be waiting for you there, and wanted you to know that she loves you, very much. And that she is going to miss you until she can be together with you again."

Mr. Thompson shuddered, the words stinging against the pain already in his heart. "How do you know? How can you know?"

"I just know it in my heart," Kaden said confidently.

Mr. Thompson stood, rubbing at his eyes and trying to gather his self-control. "My sister is going to arrange the f-funeral. I'll tell her to send you the information if you'd like to attend."

"Thank you."

"No. Thank you for being her friend. She liked and admired you a lot, Kaden. You were all she ever talked about whenever I came to see her. I'm so glad she met you." Mr. Thompson gripped Kaden's shoulder and squeezed it, conveying the rest of his emotions without words before slowly trudging out of the hospital, bent like an old man.

Kaden rubbed at the ache in his chest and walked to the elevator, taking it down to the bottom floor, where Logan waited for him. Shea welcomed him home, along with Charlie and Mantacor. It still pained him to know that Becca was gone, but he still worked hard at walking without the cane. He attended the funeral a few days after he'd returned home with Logan by his side. He couldn't keep from crying, even though he knew Becca would be mad at him. The father gave him a picture of Kaden and Becca taken together one day at the hospital, before she'd become severely ill. He treasured it and kept it in his wallet.

The day he could walk without the cane, he went to "see" her, to tell her about his accomplishment. He sat down close to her gravestone, tracing the letters of her name: *Rebecca Beverly Thompson, the light of a father's world.* "Hey, Becca. I miss you. A lot. Sometimes I stop what I'm doing to think about you. Guess what? I don't have to use the cane anymore. I can walk without it. I wish you were here to see it, but I know wherever you are, you can see me and know that I'm doing okay."

He looked down at the grass, and pulled at some of the weeds growing around the headstone. "I just wanted to say thank you, because if it hadn't been for you, I might not have had the strength to walk again. You were guiding me all along."

He stood, struggling a little as he still wasn't completely steady on his feet, and gently laid the single rose he'd brought with him on the top of the headstone, smiling softly. "I'll see you later, Becca."

"You ready to go home?" Kaden turned to find Logan standing nearby, waiting patiently for him. It seemed as though Logan was always patiently waiting for him to catch up, and he smiled broadly, rushing over to Logan's side. He slipped his arm through Logan's and smiled up at him.

"Let's go home." They walked back to the truck where Logan opened his door for him before climbing into the driver's side. The cowboy picked up his hand and entwined their fingers after starting the vehicle and slowly pulling away from the cemetery.

Kaden turned his head to the side to study the larger man's profile, the sun flashing off his features as the trees around them would cover and uncover the sun. He could see the contentment in Logan's face, and the looks of affection and love that the cowboy tossed his way. Logan's lips curved up slightly at the corner, and he glanced over at Kaden. "What? Do I have something on my face?"

"No, it's not that. Just thinking about how thankful I am."

"Thankful? For what?" Logan asked in confusion.

"For being blessed by meeting you and for you loving me," Kaden said honestly, his eyes conveying his sincerity.

Logan smiled, lifting Kaden's hand to his mouth and placing a gentle kiss on the boy's knuckles. "I should be the one who's thankful. If not for my cousin, I'd have never met you, and my world would still be dark without the moon to light my path."

Kaden flushed at the mushy words that Logan used, but his eyes flooded with love for the larger cowboy. "Let's hurry home, because I'm starving."

"But we just had a huge breakfast!" Logan exclaimed in astonishment, looking at Kaden.

"I didn't say I was starving for food," Kaden teased, winking at Logan.

It took Logan a moment to process what the younger man implied, but once it hit, he threw his head back and laughed. Loudly. "It's only been eight hours," he taunted, grinning at the flush that overtook Kaden's features. "But if you can't wait until we get back to the ranch, there's this motel out on the interstate…." he trailed off suggestively.

Kaden nodded enthusiastically and shifted over to start kissing on Logan's neck. It still amazed him how well things had turned out for him in Montana, but he wouldn't change anything for the world. He thanked God that he'd taken the job and that Logan had known to touch him gently, leaving him with the taste for more.

Epilogue

Music blared through the booth as he stood there, and Kaden couldn't help but have a sense of pride while watching the band playing behind the glass. Nothing could compare to hearing his lyrics actually being sung. Arms wrapped around his waist from behind, and he leaned back into the embrace with a wide grin. Logan's voice caressed his ear. "It sounds great."

Kaden nodded and reveled in all the good things that had happened to him in the past year and a half. Logan had moved him into his room at the ranch, and not long after had discovered his lyrics notebook. The cowboy had raved over them, encouraging him to put them out there for the world to see. It had taken some time before he'd come up with the courage to show them to other people, but it wasn't long until they were snapped up by a high-profile band and now he stood here, listening to them being sung by an artist whose voice compared to a beautiful summer sunset on the ranch.

The band was recording at the moment, and he saw the lead singer wink at him through the glass. A flush dusted over his cheeks, and he felt Logan's arms tighten around him. Mitchell Kingsley had been hitting on him from day one, trying to lure him away from Logan. It had almost caused a fist fight to break out between the two men, but Kaden made it clear to Mitchell that only one man held his heart, the one currently holding him. He tilted his head back and wrinkled his nose up at Logan. "You don't have to be jealous, Logan. I already told him that my heart only belongs to one person."

"That better be me," Logan growled into his ear, and Kaden laughed, shaking his head.

"How can you still be so unsure about me, Logan? We've been together for two years now, and you are everything to me." Kaden turned around in Logan's embrace and looked up at the man who'd saved him in so many ways. The band transitioned into the next song, and the words spilling from Mitchell's lips drifted over them both. "Besides, I don't write a song for just anyone, you know."

Logan smiled tenderly down into the violet eyes gazing up at him and stroked his thumb over Kaden's cheeks. Words from the song dug into his heart, burrowing deep, and sending reassurance to him. Kaden had blossomed in such a way in the past year and a half that Logan couldn't help but be afraid other people would see that and try to take him away. Like the one singing his love's songs at that very moment. He rubbed his nose against Kaden's and pulled him closer, drawing his lips lightly over the younger man's before leaning back. "How much longer until we can go home?" he asked.

"This is the last session, and besides, I don't have to be here. I already know how they sound. This is just the recording session." Kaden grinned at Mitchell in the recording room, and the man's voice trembled a little at the utter happiness on the kid's face.

Mitchell had tried everything to swing Kaden's attention to him, drawn to the younger man's innocence and beauty. He'd been astounded at the teen's ability to write lyrics, and the depth of emotion behind them. It struck a chord in his heart, bringing forth the urge to protect and hold the smaller man. But nothing he did could draw Kaden's attention away from the big cowboy, much to his disappointment. He struck the last chord on his guitar and watched the two men in the booth as the last note faded away to silence. He could see the affection and love between them. It made him ache for someone of his own. It had been a long time since he'd had a relationship that lasted for longer than a month.

Sighing, he stood up and made his way into the booth to say goodbye to the younger man and the cowboy. "Great session, guys," he called out to his band mates.

"Kaden," he shouted as he entered the booth, smiling in pleasure. He hugged the younger man tightly before stepping back to gaze down at him. "I hope that we did justice to your songs, man."

"You did!" Kaden exclaimed excitedly. "I loved every one of them. Your voice is perfect for the words. I'm just so amazed that you chose my songs over the ones professionals write."

"You are a professional, Kaden." Mitchell smiled at him. "Your lyrics have something to them that will touch the lives of thousands of people everywhere. Don't stop writing, because in a year, I'm coming back for more!"

"Great! But keep in touch more often than that. Otherwise I'll think you only want me for my words," Kaden teased, his eyes sparkling with laughter.

"You should know better than that by now," Mitchell growled, but he stepped back a little further when he saw the anger that darkened the big cowboy's features. "I'll have them send you the CD once it's done. Have a safe flight back to Montana." With that, he left the booth to join his mates again.

Logan grabbed Kaden's hand and started to drag him from the booth. "Whoa. Slow down, Logan," Kaden protested.

"I just want to get you alone. Now. Before I explode," Logan ground out as he continued to pull Kaden along behind him to the elevators. Once inside, he yanked Kaden into his arms and brought their lips together in a heated and passionate kiss. Their mouths were trained for each other, knowing exactly how to move and how to part to please the other. Logan's hands slid down Kaden's slim back to cup his ass, pulling him tighter against him and grinding their stiff flesh together. Kaden gasped under Logan's mouth, and he moaned at the friction of his jeans rubbing against him.

"Logan," he pleaded, his head lolling back as Logan's mouth left a blazingly hot trail to his throat. Kaden's hands slid up into Logan's mane and held on for dear life, his chest heaving with his panting breath. "We... ah... shouldn't be doing this here," he moaned, loving the feeling of the hard body pinning him to the elevator wall.

"I'm dying for you, Kaden," Logan sighed, his teeth nipping at the skin twitching from the boy's pulse pounding beneath the flesh. "I need to be inside you, to feel you, to touch you. So deep."

Kaden's eyes slid closed at Logan's words, and he tugged Logan's lips to his, capturing whatever else the bigger man would possibly say. Caught in the heat of the moment, they were unaware of the elevator stopping or the doors sliding open. A woman gasping behind them brought them out of their trance, and Kaden grinned cheekily up at Logan. "I think we've been caught."

Logan chuckled, his broad chest rumbling with the sound as he helped Kaden walk from the elevator, tipping his hat at the group of women who stood there. One of the women giggled, and the others just gave the two of them affronted looks as they passed by. Kaden had grown to be more accepting of people's censure and had learned to ignore it. His playful side had grown as he had grown, and Logan couldn't be happier or prouder of the way the younger man had progressed. "Let's go back to our hotel room," he said suggestively, and Kaden smirked up at him.

190

"I don't know," he replied with an indecisive sigh. "I mean, there is a lot of sightseeing that I wanted to do still."

A growl worked its way out of Logan's throat, and he leaned down to rumble into Kaden's ear. "If you don't get your butt in that limo and get us back to that hotel room, I'm going to take you up against this building and be damned everyone who wants to watch."

The violet eyes widened, and he laughed huskily and a bit hesitantly. Kaden wasn't so sure that Logan wouldn't do just that. "Fine," he said with a roll of his eyes, and he thanked the driver holding the door open to the limo before slipping inside.

The instant the door shut, Logan hit the button to roll up the privacy window and had Kaden pinned to the soft seat of the limo. Over a year ago, that move would have had Kaden quivering in terror, now it only left him quivering in anticipation. Logan's hand found its way beneath the hem of Kaden's shirt to caress the slightly rough skin of his stomach, and his lips latched onto Kaden's ear, suckling hotly. Kaden moaned and sucked in a deep breath when he felt Logan's fingers roaming over his nipples. "Logan, please," he whimpered, gripping Logan's muscled back.

"Please what, little one?" Logan's hot breath slithered over the sensitive skin of his neck, sending a shiver of pleasure through his thin body.

"Please don't tease me," he groaned, arching off the seat as far as Logan's body would allow.

"You don't want me to do this?" Logan licked the outer ridges of the tantalizing ear. "Or this?" He slipped the tip of his tongue inside Kaden's ear, ripping a moan of pleasure from the younger man. "Not even this?" His hand slid down to cup Kaden through his jeans, flexing his fingers to massage the hot and heavy flesh beneath the confining fabric.

"Logan!" Kaden mewled, his breath panting from his lungs, and he decided to extract his own form of torture. His hands moved down to grip at Logan's hips, thrusting one of his legs between Logan's. He started to massage the bulge in the cowboy's jeans with his thigh, and he felt the shudder rip through the larger man. He grinned in satisfaction and murmured, "I can be just as wicked as you."

Logan knew that Kaden had him in the palm of his slender hand, and he would do anything that his little one wanted. He sat up, bringing Kaden with him to settle him into his lap. As his lips claimed Kaden's, his fingers nimbly slid the button of Kaden's jeans from its hole and the zipper parted easily, sliding down to its base. Logan worked his hand inside Kaden's jeans and caressed him through his underwear. His pulse leaped with lust at the small gasps that Kaden released as he massaged, rubbed, and squeezed gently. The cock beneath his palm felt hot and hard, driving his own passion through the roof. "You are so hot," Logan said huskily.

"I... umm...." Kaden's voice cracked when he felt Logan's fingers brush over the tip of his cock. "This isn't... mmm... the best... p-place for this!" He tried to find the energy to halt Logan's ministrations, but his hand remained gripping the hard muscled shoulder.

"But your expression is so sexy," Logan moaned, slowly lifting Kaden's hard prick free from the jeans. The cool air of the limo hit the heated shaft, sending a shiver through Kaden. "And I can't wait until we get back to the hotel to touch you, to taste you." With those words, his hand gripped the younger man's straining cock and began to stroke the soft, silky cage over the iron bar beneath it.

Kaden's eyes were half-slits as his breath wheezed between his parted lips. Lightning zipped through his body, connected to that calloused palm sliding easily over his dick. He watched

192

Logan's expression as the man watched his hand caressing him. He leaned forward and buried his face in Logan's neck, suckling at the salty flesh under his lips. Trembling, he felt his passion rising, pushing for the surface like a diver beneath the ocean. "Logan... oh...."

Logan moved quickly, placing Kaden on the seat beside him and diving down to take just the pink tip onto his tongue, closing his lips around it as Kaden lost it. The small cry that Kaden let out pleased him more than anything else in the world. He swallowed greedily, allowing not even a drop to escape his lips. He used his tongue to clean his lover before moving up and over Kaden. The boy's eyes were closed, and his lips were parted on a gasping breath. Logan's heart swelled at the sight before him, and he lifted his hand to brush a lock of black hair back from his sweat-dampened forehead. "You are more beautiful to me than the mountains on our ranch."

Kaden's hand rose up to trace the deep scar that ran the line of his cheek, and his eyes opened with uncertainty shining deep inside him. "Even with this?"

"That is part of you, Kaden. Everything about you is beautiful." Logan leaned down and placed a gentle kiss upon the scar, drawing his lips down the length from where it started at the corner of his eye to the end at the corner of his mouth. "I love you."

The younger man's lips curled into a contented smile, and Kaden's thin arms wrapped around his shoulders. "I love you too."

The limo came to a stop, and they hurriedly fixed themselves up before the driver could open the door. The moment they entered their suite, Logan stripped the clothes from Kaden's body. Once the smaller man was naked, he lifted Kaden into his arms and carried him to the bedroom. Kaden laughed softly and ran his fingers through the mane of golden hair. "I always likened you to a lion. Did you know that?"

Logan gave him a questioning look as he set him on the bed. His eyes drank in the sight of his lover lying among the silk sheets, innocent yet sinful. "Your eyes reminded me of cat's eyes. And your hair is like the golden fur of a lion," Kaden explained, holding out his arms for Logan to join him.

It still made Logan's breath hitch at the sheer beauty stretched out before him, and he slowly shed his own clothing before accepting Kaden's embrace. He breathed in deeply, dragging Kaden's scent into his lungs. He leaned close to him, pressing his lips to the corner of Kaden's mouth, moving upward to the tip of his nose, and higher still to his eyelids. As he dropped a light kiss on each, he proclaimed, "You are the only thing I live for. My life was empty until that day. There is nothing I wouldn't do to make you happy."

Kaden smiled tenderly and reached up to caress Logan's cheek, watching in amusement as the large cowboy leaned into his touch like a giant cat. "You make me happy just by being with you." He slid his right leg up and around to hook behind his back. "Make love to me, Logan. Please," he begged, and he felt Logan tremble with emotion.

Their lips met in a soft and sweet kiss as Logan prepared Kaden for him. Kaden sighed with pleasure as he felt Logan entering his body, sliding his other leg around his waist to bring their bodies closer together. Logan's eyes never left Kaden's as he slowly began to move, pushing his hips forward, spearing deep inside him. Kaden gripped Logan's shoulders, digging his fingers into the muscles beneath them, reveling in the intimate connection. No words were uttered, their bodies undulating together in a languid and loving dance. Logan dipped his head low and captured Kaden's mouth with his own. Nothing existed outside of the two of them. Gentle sighs of pleasure, lingering touches of reverence, and tender kisses of affection were all that they were.

Kaden gripped Logan frantically, letting out a small cry of ecstasy as his fluids spilled between their bodies. His snug entrance tightened even further around Logan's invading flesh, demanding the other man's essence, milking it from his body. Logan buried his face in the crook of Kaden's neck as he exploded, moaning deeply at the almost sucking sensation of the younger man's body. Finally, they fell still. Their bodies quivered from the overload of sensations, and Kaden drew a shaky hand through the dark blond strands of Logan's hair. Unwilling to break the silence, they lay there, merely savoring the feel of one another.

It could have been seconds, or maybe even hours later, before Logan slipped from Kaden's body and slid to the side, gathering the younger man close. He rested his chin atop Kaden's dark head and sighed in contentment. "I can't believe that Shea is getting married in two weeks. It feels like I'm losing my baby sister."

Snuggling closer, Kaden wrinkled his nose. "You're not losing your baby sister. You're gaining a brother. Besides, I've never seen her so happy. She really loves him."

"Well, Tyson better take care of her, or I'll have to kick his ass down to the honky-tonk and back again," Logan snarled.

Laughter bubbled up inside Kaden's throat, and his body fairly shook with it. "I think that Shea can take care of herself, Logan. She's a strong woman and knows what she wants. Besides, Ty's a great guy."

"I'm looking forward to going back to the ranch tomorrow. And you aren't leaving it again, ever. You're too tempting, and someone might try to steal you away again." Logan's emerald eyes darkened with jealousy at the memory of Kingsley trying at every turn to catch Kaden's interest.

"Stop," Kaden chastised gently. "I don't want anyone else. You are the one I love, Logan. No one will ever be able to steal me away."

The expression in Logan's eyes softened, and he pulled him firmly into his body, running a hand down Kaden's thin back. His palm brushed over the scar at the base of his spine, and a shudder wound its way down his own. He'd almost lost him once. That day would haunt him for the rest of his life. He tried so hard not to smother Kaden, not to keep him from living, but it took a lot of his strength to not lock him away from the world. "I cannot bear the thought of losing you, Kaden. You are more to me than my own life. Without you in it, it wouldn't be worth living. I love you so much."

A sigh of affection drifted from Kaden's lips, and he smiled as he pulled back to be able to look up at Logan. "I'm not going anywhere. You are my home. I can't wait to get back to the ranch, either. Mantacor must be so lonely without me."

"You and that horse. I still can't get anywhere near him, but you… you can do almost anything to that horse, and he lets you." Logan sighed. It still frustrated him to know that Mantacor would have nothing to do with him.

"I know that bothers you," Kaden admitted softly. "But sometimes it's not always easy to gain the trust of a frightened creature. One day he will learn to trust you, Logan. I have faith in him."

Logan grunted but didn't say anything. It had taken him a long time to gain Kaden's complete trust. The fear had slowly receded and been replaced by love and affection. Logan looked down at where Kaden's right hand rested against his chest, his eyes centering on the ring that graced his ring finger. For Christmas last year, he'd given the younger man a promise ring. He hadn't expected Kaden to cry, and he'd been shocked as he'd watched the violet eyes he loved so much fill up with tears that slowly trickled over. Only Kaden had had this huge smile on his face, and a second later, he had launched himself at Logan, catching him by surprise. He wore a similar ring on his hand, showing his own promise to the younger man.

They lay in silence, just listening to each other breathe. Logan's thoughts turned to the reason Kaden had found the strength to walk again, and he broke the quiet by asking, "Do you still think about her?"

Kaden knew who he was referring to and nodded. "Yeah. I do. I wish things had been different, and she'd lived. But I know she's happy where she is. I talk to her father every once in a while. He's remarried to a widow with two children. He says that they've helped him to heal, a lot. But he still misses her. I suppose he always will. It's not right that a father should outlive his child."

"Do you think…." Logan hesitated, not sure if he should bring it up or not.

"What?" Kaden looked at him in question, his brow furrowed in a small frown. Logan had never been reticent about talking to him about anything.

"Would you possibly want to adopt a child someday?" Logan held his breath. He'd been thinking about it more and more as each day passed. To be able to provide a wonderful and loving home to another child. Someone perhaps like Kaden, whose childhood had been cut short.

Kaden's eyes widened, and he sucked in a breath in surprise. "I thought you didn't want to have children."

"I used to think like that. Only because I didn't want to bring another being into this world and have them suffer what I went through. But nothing would feel more right than raising a child with you."

Silence reigned for a moment, and Logan shifted in discomfort, wondering if maybe Kaden didn't want to, but then a beautiful smile broke out over Kaden's lips. "I would love to raise a child with you, Logan. I think you'd make a wonderful father.

Even if you don't give yourself enough credit for it."

Logan released the breath he had been holding and crushed Kaden to him. As he spoke, his breath rustled the strands of hair at the edge of Kaden's forehead, tickling the younger man slightly. "We can start looking once we get back home. I think that Shea will be happy to know she's going to be an auntie."

Kaden couldn't believe how blissful his life had turned out. Shadows still lurked inside his mind, trying to convince him that this wouldn't last, but he never let them take hold. His heart wouldn't allow it. He was part of a family now and couldn't let those shadows defeat him. It had taken him a long time to find the happiness he had now, and he refused to let it go without a fight. He heard Logan's breathing begin to even out as the large cowboy slipped into sleep, and he snuggled closer, closing his eyes in peace when the man's arms instinctively tightened, sheltering him and protecting him from any nightmares that might try to threaten him. The sky had just begun to darken as he drifted off to sleep himself, the stars shining through the curtain, blanketing the earth and lighting the way for those who still needed it.

J.R. LOVELESS is a native Floridian who spends her days in an office physically but mentally is frolicking between the pages of her imagination. Writing has been a lifelong passion that escaped from her in the midst of life until she discovered yaoi. After following breadcrumbs of the anime style, she discovered a forum dedicated to the world of yaoi. Inspired, she tried her own hand at M/M romances, spending hours building worlds of her own with the newfound support of other forum members. She can never write enough of the electrifying emotions that blaze across the hearts and souls of her characters.

She is a self-confessed *Dr. Who* addict with a spastic dog and a neurotic cat for companions on her long journey through the many chapters of her life. One day she hopes to visit far off places and have grand adventures like those of the characters in her stories.

You can contact her at jrloveless@gmail.com.

Western Romance from DREAMSPINNER PRESS

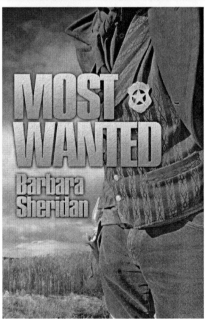

http://www.dreamspinnerpress.com

Romance from DREAMSPINNER PRESS

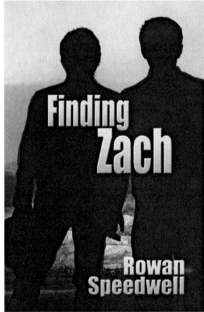

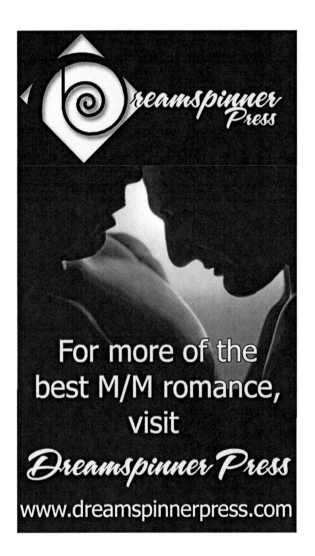

LaVergne, TN USA
20 October 2010
201545LV00007B/154/P